# MONTAGE DOMNIK

# New Stories
# and Poems
# from Dominica

# MONTAGE DOMNIK

# New Stories and Poems from Dominica

VOLUME 1

Waitukubuli Writers: "Crafting authentic literature from Dominica for readers at home and around the world."
www.facebook.com/waitukubuliwriters

© River Ridge Press, Dominica 2021
ISBN: 978-976-95795-4-5
www.facebook.com/RiverRidgePressDominica

Cover art, typesetting, layout & design by Giselle Laurent
Printed by ImprintDigital.com

# MONTAGE DOMNIK

# New Stories and Poems from Dominica

## POEMS

## SHORT STORIES

## COVID-19 POEMS

# Publisher's Note

Long before Spanish explorers christened the island Dominica, indigenous Kalinago Indians called their homeland "Waitukubuli," meaning "Tall is Her Body." It is an accurate description of the most mountainous island in the Eastern Caribbean. Nestled between the French islands of Guadeloupe and Martinique, Dominica rises up out of the sea in a series of volcanic peaks to a height of nearly 5,000 feet. Likewise, the title of this ground-breaking anthology, *Montage Domnik: New Stories and Poems from Dominica*, describes not only the lush physical landscape of the island, but also the soaring, fertile imaginations of its contributors.

This colorful collection serves as a platform to expose and preserve new work from twenty-four of Dominica's most energetic writers at home and in the diaspora. As many of the themes are divergent from the accepted worldview, voices that have never been heard are showcased within its pages. In dialect, standard English, and Creole patois, these poems and stories address a wide variety of relevant Caribbean themes. The quest for cultural preservation and the importance of family values is examined. The role of sports, the influence of folklore and superstition, migration, crime, and natural disaster is explored. And it is all presented from an island-based perspective rather than through a distant spyglass!

In a rapidly changing world, it's important for small places to cherish their unique cultural heritage and hold tight to the values of family and community that bind them together. Climate change and rising sea levels have already negatively impacted infrastructure and food security in Dominica. Category 5 Hurricane Maria reminded islanders that if they intend to stay afloat, literally and figuratively, they must be resilient. More recently, COVID-19 effectively eradicated tourism. Nowadays, it's imperative to adapt in order to survive. But as Peter Tosh asked the downpresser man over forty years ago, 'Where you gonna run to?' The question seems more valid now than ever in light of global warming, coronavirus, and the social and racial unrest overseas.

Waitukubuli Writers, the group that assembled this body of work, is a treasure trove of poets and writers from Dominica who cherish their island and its culture. I urge everyone who reads this collection to embrace its diversity and ignore the influences that minimalise literature from beyond the mainstream. Island books matter, and the time has come to liberate our creative voices in print.

I wish you happy reading.

Kristine Simelda
River Ridge Press, Dominica

# Epigram

*'Savage the winds rake:*
*yet the bamboo does not break.'*

Phyllis Shand Allfrey,
"Return," It Falls into Place,
2004 Papillote Press

# POEMS

## Of Rivers

We ran in the streets naked
And sometimes topless
Needless to say
We cared not about sunburns
Or broken bones.

We climbed trees
With branches that were strong.
We threw stones
At the ones that
Could not support our weight.

We were children of the river.
We skipped off stones,
Drumming and playing air guitar.
Everything was fine
Once we had the river to run to.

We were young.
Never thought
We'd grow up or grow old.
We survived the test of time
But the rivers did not.
They are mostly streams now.
A trickle, in most instances.

ANELLA D. SHILLINGFORD is a member of Waitukubli Writers and an emerging writer. She is the author of *Bonfire*, a book of poems available on Amazon. She has a monthly blog, where she shares personal experiences with a unique spin. Anella is also a secondary school teacher in Portsmouth.

# Mama Ever Told You

Mama ever told you to
be careful with your eggs?
She ever told you don't
put them all in one basket?
Or don't count them before they hatch?

Mama ever told you
Don't wear your heart on your sleeve?
She ever told you never love him
more than he loves you?
Or don't love him at all?

Mama never told you
Never say never?
She never told you never tell a lie
Or never swear?
Never spill your guts.

Mama ever told you
Tell the truth but not all of it.
Be careful with your secrets.
There's always a fly on the wall
and bushes have ears.

Mama ever told you
To make haste while the sun still shines?
She ever told you to go fast and come back fast?
She ever told you to cry and finish fast?
Or don't make her spit dry before you come back?

Mama ever told you
That life would be hard?
She ever told you nothing
would be handed to you?
Or nothing was free?

Mama ever told you
Fairytales aren't real?
She ever told you that
there are no happy endings
Or prince charmings?

All the lessons mama taught us
And stories she told us
Under candle light
In the yard we shared with
All her relatives.

How she'd rise before the cock crowed
How'd she'd stand knee-deep
In the sun-kissed water
Bent over sun-bathed grey stones
To "chocho"* our clothes.

All the lessons we learnt from mama.
And we're still learning.
But here's what she never told us:
She's still learning the tricks of the trade,
Because no one was there to teach her.

She's still learning her own lessons.
She's still lighting her way through darkness.
She's still learning to rise after every fall.
Because, grown-ups make mistakes too.
Did mama ever tell us that?

*chocho = colloquial term for
hand-washing washing

# Fried Plantains

I'm not sure why I tend to think
Fried plantains are the delight of every Caribbean
  man

Maybe it somehow grew from our roots
Or maybe it's just my personal affair with this
  somewhat unusual fruit
Man, I love fried plantains

I love them plain or with a little sugar sprinkled on
  top
I love them cold or hot
They go down well with a hot cup of "cacao" tea

Ice cold "Kubuli"
With some cucumber salad or salt fish on the side
There's no combination that I haven't tried

The sun could be bursting through the pleated
  curtains
The rain could be banging on the galvanized roof
I enjoy them anyway and that's the truth

I have fried plantains whether I'm hungry or filled
Sad or happy
Sick or healthy
It doesn't matter how I feel

Nothing has ever stopped me from eating fried
  plantains
Except for that day

You stopped talking to me

That day fried plantains lay cold
And alone
Craving human contact
Struggling with the fact

EDD ELICK, member of Waitukubuli Writers, is from the coastal village of Fond Colé. He combines his passion for poetry and film, with his education, to create content for self-expression that has garnered thousands of views across his social media platforms. Find his work at: eddelickpoetry on YouTube or Facebook.

That suddenly it's an unwanted snack
And oh how it hurt my heart
To have to dump fried plantains in the garbage bin

My dearest don't you ever do that again
Cause man, I love fried plantains.

## Stronghold

She was a stronghold for everyone
and they loved her for it
She was a stronghold for everyone and they didn't
  deserve it
She held them up when they could not
She comforted all within her walls
Gave them shelter and kept them warm
A place to weather the nastiest storms
But when her beams got bent,
And her energy spent
Poked holes in her ceiling,
Her exterior paint peeling
Where was her stronghold then?
Vanished, along with lovers, soul mates and
  supposed friends.

LEONA JEREMIAH is a 26-year-old young woman with a passion for written expression. From a very young age she developed a deeply rooted love for poetry and has been writing ever since. She is also a Pharmacy Technician, youth leader and an avid humanitarian.

# Changing Seasons

My Life's nothing like shades and blue curtains
My shields see-through, the sun bursts inside
When it rains it falls, it pours, it pours
It wets my floors, my floor's floorboards
I don't normally let my windows open but you promised
 a forecast of autumn
You promised a spring of wind and light, to lift me up
 and lull me to sleep at night...
But the rain is what you thrive in
You just put up a front to get a way in
Thunderstorms are your best friend; Tsunamis,
 Earthquakes, Hurricane Trade Winds...
How was I to know you breed disaster?
How was I to know the detriment that would follow
 soon after?
How was I to weather those storms unprepared?
How was I to breathe in your polluted air?

# Dialects of Brown

I am stuck in the dialectics of brown
Ruminations of who and where, I come from.
Neither accepting of black nor white
Always caught up in the social plight

It is an argument, serpentine
Confusing turns, leaves the mind blind
To realities of identity
Who I am versus who should I be?

Should I claim black, who rejects
Should I claim white, a history to accept
Should we be mulatto, of our own
But the degrees of disparity, leaves us prone

Am I defined by colour or hair?
I'd like to say my soul, but that is another affair
People are limited by what they can see
Who you are is secondary to who they perceive you
  to be

"Oh you so light, you have couleur"
"All yu lucky, you have nice hair"
"Look at your nose, so well-shaped"
These are statements of minds raped

But dissension is but, surface deep
The negatives thrown, makes the eyes weep
As you evolve from the shelters of youth
Confusion reigns, in your search for truth

Proudly, I hold onto my father's name
Even if the inheritance is shrouded in shame
Legitimacy was always in question
It is the obsession, the underlying aggression

RONALD DESCHAMPS, from the early days of the People's Action Theatre, participated in stage plays, dance interpretations, and radio dramas. He collaborated as an illustrator for various writers, is the founder of Domnichen Poetic Circle Facebook platform, and continues to work as an architect/designer in NYC.

Brown is the new racial fashionista
Yet to some, a social pariah
Even amongst ourselves, we are misunderstood
Confusion, delusion is just under the hood

In the Caribbean, my history is Mulatto
The word itself derogatory, so you know
I am not seen as a whole, but a fragment
the deconstruction of which was in the statement

I have been called:
bèké pauvre,
bèké la riviere,
malesway
chabeh
octaroon
creole
mestizo
zambo
half-breed,
biracial
multiracial
interracial

Children of perplexing inheritance
Black you accept, white keep your distance
But the confusion never subsides
And life becomes tumultuous rides

I am not mad. I know who I am
I am a unique expression of God's plan
It is the spirit than makes me human
I am not just colour, I trust you understand

# A Powerful Storm—Faith, Hope, Love

We were in the path of the storm,
Very powerful—not the norm.
It would have sorely crushed us all.
Thank God! We came through standing tall.
Our faith—tested to the limit.
Hope sustained us. We survived it.
Some risked their lives to save others;
Proud sons of fathers and mothers.
For those we lost we feel deep pain.
Faith gives us hope, we'll meet again.
We had much love and care before;
In distress we embraced them more.
Nature is bouncing back we see.
We will recover wait and see.
With unity we'll reach our goal,
Each one a part that makes the whole.

VIDA WILSON TOUSSAINT, born in Guyana in 1954, worked at a credit union and was employed as a teacher while raising three children in Dominica. Her desire is to write poetry that sends a positive message for troubled times, and she believes it's important to live a simple, charitable life no matter the circumstances.

# Her Dog

The dog's bearing has grown forlorn, His eyes the
  waning moon.
I cannot touch it anymore, My fingers recoil
At the memory of the bones

And every step on the dry bamboo leaves

A replay of drying breath, Belaboured.

The yard
Is now strewn with the brown signs

Of energy in transition

The Heliconias, their bright orange

Once a medal of good housekeeping, are no more. The
  Dog comes over, its gait
Is arthritic and painful to watch. It is now wrapped
In a deep silence

That seems to have eaten away at the once glossy coat

Which in the past, shone

Deep red in the tropical sun

As it ran about to its mistress' command

That was then; now its head

Is hung heavy. I cannot cross the divide

Between us

Nor the unspoken weight

That knots at my throat cutting off my voice

Nor can I hold his gaze

As he with great effort stares up at me with eyes
  brimming over with questions

CURTIS
CLARENDON
is a retired banker
and poet who has
won short story
competitions in
Dominica. He is a
member of The
People's Action
Theatre, and his
play, *Shellie*, was
accepted in 2008 by
the Martin E. Segal
Theatre Center,
CUNY. In 2016, he
directed the film
*Pretending Reality*,
produced by La
Cour Des Arts De La
Dominique.

To evade him and the depression

With which he is now burdened I flee into the house

That no longer has a sense

Of home

Though the same walls and shapes are there

The living room, her sunken cheeks, is now hollow and
spare

Its shadows now grown heavier

Though there are no curtains anymore

Their colourful absence will mean the fading into
forgetfulness the liturgical seasons

Just as the "lamp Vierge" of the eyes fixed into eternity

Has been disconnected

So too the rooms

Even the kitchen is hung with a strange coldness

With the once fiery stoves disturbingly quiet.

The walls are bare of the memorabilia of the past, of
connection.

There is no need for them, for her absence

Is noted everywhere; the windows stripped of their
curtains

The cutlery, still and packed away

No hymns are being hummed

In her fashion: bits and pieces, interspersed with
instructions and thoughts.

No more is the heart beat that once coupled these
  rooms

Making a home within these four walls. And the dog
Poor thing

Unable to climb the one step from the living room to
  the dining room

Waits in his gloom

Waits in vain for her

Waits for her to get out of the sick-room, He awaits her
  call to cross over
Burdened in expressing the grief for us all.

# My Mother

Is it not tempting to envision Mother Earth as
 classically beautiful, fine, willow in stature and ever
 loving and gentle
Maybe just a little hurt; a small nothing from our
 childish carelessness.
A bruise, She supremely able to overcome through
 Her sweet stable nature our fickle destruction.
But NO!
Not my Mother!
No woman who could bear me could be willowy or
 fine in stature...nooooo
She would need a strong broad back to carry Her
 swelling belly
Firm sinewed legs to walk the distance to the fields
 of war and glory
Powerful arms tapering to loving yet stern hands to
 carry me and school me
A mind able to encompass the Nations of her loins.
Her inner self; indomitable but humble. Constantly
 hungry for Life, Beauty and Truth
She strides forth with patience, fortitude and a will
 unseen, indeed, unknown by the mulish scion she
 has birthed.

My Mother

ANTONIA
HARRIS,
born in 1972, is a
mother of two
daughters and
currently resides in
Dominica. She has
always had a
passion for writing
and literature, and
she uses the
platform as a
release for coping
with life's
struggles. Through
her work, she
hopes to connect
with others facing
similar situations,
so they know they
are not alone.

# Farm Hands

Madame
Doh watch me dem kinda way
I know wah yuh thinking, that I'm good-for-nothing,
   dirty ole man
But mi serious, mi just want a likkle job to hold me up
I see yuh turn up yuh nose when yuh look at mi hands
But after years of toiling the land, I'm proud of these
   hands
These hands, they make me into ah man!
They send mi chirren to school, and make sure they
   always had food
Wasn't always the best, no, in fact, far from what you
   consider "good food"
I couldn't afford steak and lasagne
But their bellies still did full with balaw season up with
   greens from the garden, some cush-cush and banana
And what better to wash that down, than a lime squash
   with brown sugar!
Years of digging in soil, and carrying load and water,
   make mi hands them look something like a tractor
But every line, cut and bruise on them, fill me with
   pride and sometimes even laughter
Even the dirt which did stain under my finger nails
Carry their own story, which I remember on quiet days
I used to hide as a little boy, because I was shame of my
   family background
While everybody else was in summer school and
   hopping big plane
I was in mi father garden picking pepper and cutting
   sugar cane
And many days *formi rouge* would end up in places
   where the sting felt worse!
See me hopping and jumping, and trying to hold back
   the curse!

MICHELLE ALLYSHIA BELLE, a Dominican currently residing in China, has been exposed to a kaleidoscope of people, cultures, and life experiences. As a young black woman, her writing is seasoned with the rhythmic vibrancy of her African-Caribbean roots while capturing a kaleidoscope of universal thoughts, fantasies, hopes and fears.

We was poor yes, but Daddy made sure we had respect
And Mammy always encouraged us to do our best
So, I did try to raise my chirren with the same kinda
  mind
I send them to school yes, but they had to know the
  value of every dime
"Do with what you have, and never steal or kill for what
  you do not"
And a good lick every now and then when words were
  not enough!
I had a tamarind whip, soak up in sea water
I hear now they call that child abuse
Well at that time, it didn't have nobody to arrest me for
  that
So every now and then they would get a good lickin' in
  their backside
No child under my roof could backslide
All ah dem big now, they go school and get big job
They do what I never had chance to do, they did make
  me proud
The last one leave after wte put their mother in the
  ground
Look I have their pictures in my pocket
All of them overseas but they busy man, I understand
They tell me things tight, is why they can't visit or send
  me money
I know how it is when yuh have ah family
Mi just happy they making it okay
I'm a big man I can do for myself
So, if you give me the chance you'll see I'm a hard
  worker
Doh worry, that's just the life of a retired farmer.

## Life Lesson

He stood in a corner inspecting the wall
Onto which a small lizard had struggled to crawl
Finding amusement from the struggles it had
As his thoughts ran deeper it made him so sad
He noted the way that it struggled to gather its breath
Exhausted and beat, it appeared near its death
Its sole standing purpose was to get to the top
But try as it did, it would fumble and drop
Its rapid heartbeat made the outer skin pop
To climb the wall was a need, till he does he won't stop

This got him to thinking about the struggles of life
How a man must endure countless trials and strife
The lizard needed to find a safe place up high
Because with a cat in the house, it would certainly die
Like a man seeking survival by elevating himself
Or fall victim to society with their power and wealth
Everything existent has an order it seems
If you lay down and give up, your future light dims

A man's valiant efforts are often in vain
Causing him to feel helpless and laden with pain
Though some who persist, pick themselves up again
Forces stacked up against them just flush them like rain
As he stands and observes the lizards dismay
He remembers a time that he too was this way
Reminiscing the time when his mind went astray
Where an alcoholic wall had his career in a sway

He wanted so hard just to climb to the summit
But whenever he started to rise, bar time made him
  plummet
When he got sober he seemed to shoot like a comet
Again down he goes and drinks till he vomits
A close colleague at work who appreciated his worth
Enrolled him to rehab, a new chance for rebirth

ERWIN MITCHEL is an unpublished poet and short story writer from the remote village of Dipax, Castle Bruce. A fire fighter by profession whose favourite way to unwind is to grab a paper and pen. Next to his fiancée and two beautiful children, his greatest goal is to publish his lyrical creations.

He no longer felt he was alone on this earth
He inherited posture, gaining height, strength and
  girth

Looking down at the lizard with its last gleaming try
He knelt down beside it with a soft tender sigh
Then he lifted it up to the rafters up high
Now contented in heart, he knew it would get by
In his moment of hurt, through his torment and need
Someone caring and kind to his plight had took heed
They helped him along with a lifesaving deed
Sometimes as strong as we are, someone else needs to
  lead.

# My Smile

So you've asked, "why do I smile?"
When my troubles are stacked from seabed to sky
And try as I might I can't seem to get by
When ideas and ambitions can't lift off or fly
Should I give up, or sit back and cry?
When journeys I brave seem brilliant and bright
But the mission at hand is an unyielding fight
The friends that I see in days' blessed light
Seem to weigh down and drag me in secretive night
I smile ☺

The people I help in moments of need
Would tear off my head in self-driven greed
For my desires and fears, no one cares to take heed
But they gather to reap when I've planted a seed
That broken and tired I took time to sow
Whilst the date of the harvest is all they need know
Protagonists greet me with a heartfelt hello
But the look in their eyes is a death striking blow
I smile ☺

When colleagues and friends start rebelling bold
And family members freely prospect for gold
As if I've inherited much riches to hold
Of these negative forces I've never been told
By the ones who taught me to care and to love
As they taught me to value the most high above
I thought life was simple I'd fit in like a glove
But trials and stress caused my mind to evolve
So I smile ☺

Because I know of a comfort who's stronger than most
So I take all these trials to the heavenly host
The only true friend who I proudly boast
He has never neglected me, we've always been close
When life and its burdens bewilder my brain
And trials before me cause heartache and pain

If a simple goal seems to present a strain
And normal psyches are driven insane
I ease back and smile ☺

The message I'm sending is easy to say
At times all I need is to kneel down and pray
I never allow tension to ruin my day
Instead let him lead where my footsteps can stay
When devil's disciples seek to shake down my style
And toughen my journey—how long is the mile?
I need only think, take a rest for a while
Whilst the King takes the wheel, I can sit back and smile
☺ ☺

Jane Ulysses Grell
Prize for Poetry
goes to Gwenith
Whitford for her
poems
*Waitukubuli
Challenge* and
*Nature Island
Night Show.*
"Through these
poems, Gwenith
Whitford
effortlessly
captures the
drama of sights
and sounds,
together with an
undercurrent of
menace which
forms the essence
of a Dominican
night."

## Waitukubuli Challenge

When the trail
stretched out before her,
the distant mountains
did not reveal
the deep dark valleys
obscured by the sun
lengthy late-afternoon shadows
which prolonged the night
hiding steep slopes
and remote landslides
that would demand
the utmost of ability
and considerable agility
to manoeuvre skilfully
without slipping
and falling
over a precipice.

GWENITH
WHITFORD
is a free-lance
writer, editor,
blogger and poet
who currently
resides in Canada.
She was inspired to
write poetry during
the two decades
that she lived full-
time on Dominica.
Her adopted
country continues
to be a winter
escape, and she
looks forward to
further literary
inspiration every
visit.

# Nature Island Night Show

The harsh metallic glare
of a steamy afternoon
suddenly fades
as the sun drops into the sea.

In its place
cool blues, fiery oranges and bold reds
are followed by
silvery silhouettes and passing shadows.

This shimmering curtain
in the shade of dusk
quickly falls
at fifteen degrees north,

And is upstaged
by peeps, croaks and hoots
from nocturnal creatures
whose time has come,

For they are part of the night show,
with its breath-taking backdrop
of celestial orbs, sparkling stars
and a captivating moon

That invite spectators
to abandon cares
and cherish every moment,
while savouring the splendour

Of a Nature Island night.

## Politics: The Art

Politics and Politicking is an art
Of bringing out the best and most times the worst
In those who occupy many a public leadership post.
Today the Get rich model, is distastefully the creed,
Compared to decades past, today's pure greed.
Times past t'was service and de love of country
    approach,
But now, is degradation, war and reproach.
A life of continuous hate, dishonest competition to
    succeed
Entertained by those who present themselves; Our
    Country to lead.
Subtly unashamedly they condone and connive,
Eagerly searching to skin any opposition alive
Purposefully disguising what is true
To make anyone believe them; but definitely, not you.
Politics is really an art.

De art of using intimidation and fear
While ensuring the world believes that they care.
De art of providing a glimmer of hope
And in the same breath tightening the rope
That binds the oppressed, and the poor
While they draw big bucks ($$$) and kick Patriotism
    out of the door.

Its de art of keeping back the electorate
By policy application of divide and rule at any rate
While engaging their artistical skills mortgaging our
    money,
Expensively and extensively undermining our economy.

Meanwhile the masses are cajoled into mendicancy.

All this is done under brilliant articulation of unwritten
    policy

JULES PASCAL has won numerous awards for both English and Creole poetry. He is a former primary school teacher, a retired youth development worker, and an accredited Minister of the Gospel. In 1988, he co-authored a book of poems, *Pawol Kweyol*, and published *The Ravages of a Monster Storm on a Tropical Island* in 2019.

With strategic people dislocation and planned
  structural development
But really it is de art of staying in Government.

Politics is de art of painting a picture
Of working-class elevation, unemployment reduction
  and poverty alleviation,
But the real canvass displayed, depicts colours of party
loyalty and appreciation.
Speaking of art, the salaries they draw?
Could never account for the things they procure.
That's de art of concealment
Of de truth and that's de real political assignment.

Politics and politicking are really an art.
De art of leaders shifting the goal post,
De art of feeding electors with crumbs, after they've
  eaten the toast,
De art of infringing, denying and trampling on
  people's basic human rights
While perfecting de art of keeping your vote in their
  sight.

Oh, how the nations groan and yearn for political
  genuineness
That our youth can emulate and develop that
  consciousness
That they may develop the real art and paint a picture
Which depicts a realistic approach in preparing for
  the future,
The real art of being honest practicing integrity and
  truth
Something that our modern-day politicians, ought to
  invest in our youth.

# Behind That Bush

Behind that bush lies the unmatched beauty of God's
  creativity
Such beauty which one may not perceive
As the significance of the insignificant looking flower
Or the Amazona Parrot, sitting majestically in his
  bower.

Behind that bush can be seen
Creativity matched with colour and ingenuity
Displayed by nature, pointing to the Sovereignty
Of a Master builder and Creator.
Behind that bush doth exist
A continuous flow of communication
Between many the instinctive and unpredictable, yet
  formidable creatures.

Behind that bush the cascading water drops with such
  velocity
That the onlooker stops to explore the vicinity
Marvelling at the work of art.
Unaware
Of pairs of curiously staring eyes
Pondering whether he is friend or foe,
Considering how to face this intrusion
Either by flight or aggression.

Yes, behind that bush
The adventurous or the curious can perceive all sorts of
  things
From the tiniest ant to the biggest creature on wings.
Behind that bush lies the unthinkable
From the sharp-bladed grass to the tallest trees,
From sulphuric fumaroles to tranquil fresh water crater
  lakes
To a species of herb that can relieve all your aches.

From all that life needs such as a breath of clean gentle breeze
To hot springs and cold-water streams that would make the body freeze.

Behind that bush
Lies beauty for the artist's brush,
Imaginary lines for the writer's pen.
The perfect place for a quiet breath-taking spell
Away from the mad rush of those daily schedules of men.
Yes, behind that bush lies the remedy to make everything well
Inclusive of the wealth and well - being of the country
The path to chart our own destiny using this unsurpassed, amazing greenery
Like the fertile soil to grow our economy.

Yes, behind that bush is discovered the talents, skills, abilities and aspirations
Which make Dominica Nature Isle, the envy of many nations.
Yet, behind that bush has its share of negativity and 'bobol'
If not uprooted will cause a plummeting like the cascading Middleham Fall,
Into a pool of uncertainty and an unproductive swim downstream,
All in defiance of our Nation's dream
Of "All for each and each for all."

# SHORT STORIES

# A Toothbrush For Christmas

I shot up from my bed on the first beat of the Goat Skin Drummers. The clock on the night table said 5:45 am, and the calendar next to it read December 24, 1958— MY TENTH BIRTHDAY!

With a smile stretching from ear to ear, I rushed towards the veranda using my newly acquired authority to wake my big brother, Calvin, and my cousins Gregory and Mikey, all still asleep.

"Everybody WAKE UP!" I shouted. "Nine Morning band coming 'round the corner!"

"What? Jeff?" drooled Calvin, trying to catch his bearings.

My parents' alarm clock answered him with a loud RRRRRRRRRRinggggggg.

"The Nine Morning band," I repeated, "Today is Christmas Eve! Come fellas! Let's get on the veranda before those girls."

Mama had started her usual Wake-Up knock against the partition.

"Hurry! They're on our street already," Mama shouted, running through the passage to the veranda to join my sister Mara and cousins Colette and Fay who had slyly beaten us to the best seats on the veranda. Dad followed with a tray full of hot cocoa tea.

"The Drummers sweet, eh!" Mama sang out while doing a fancy three-step to the music.

In the glow of the dim streetlamps, the band of revellers morphed into a sea of writhing, billowing tides and currents, mesmerising and hypnotic, like the Roseau River in spate.

ALWIN BULLY is a cultural icon in Dominica—an administrator, playwright, actor, stage and costume designer, director, filmmaker, artist, and teacher. He is a family man who loves Carnival and is dedicated to the advancement of the arts in the Caribbean. Among his outstanding accomplishments is the design of the original national flag.

"Drink you rum on a Christmas morning, drink, you rum," the Chantwel, a small-bodied, spritely little woman with a voice louder than a microphone, challenged the crowd as she danced backwards facing them.

They replied with equal gusto: "Mama, drink if you drinking!" the happy band sang in chorus. "Drink you rum on a Christmas morning, drink you rum."

I can remember visualising the revellers pulling a reluctant sun over Morne Anglais as they chipped down King George V Street. In my vivid imagination, I could see puffs of clouds rolling down the dew-drenched mountainside releasing showers of liquid sunshine to wash Roseau's streets and gutters clean for this bright new day.

Mama looked at the rising sun with trepidation. "Sun rising fast; it have rain in it too," she warned. She looked up the Roseau Valley where the Boiling Lake was located. "That means we'll have to move fast to get all the Christmas chores done."

"That's why we came to help you, Aunty," said Collette.

"Well, I am so glad to hear that because," she pulled a long sheet of paper from her front pocket, "I have them all listed here, ready to be assigned to our teams."

The boys heaved a collective grand sigh.

"I know," Mama said gently, "but remember, many hands make work light."

"Too many cooks spoil de broth," Calvin hissed dryly.

Mama ignored him and carried on gallantly. "Here's the list," she said as she distributed copies to everyone giving detailed instructions as to how the tasks should be completed.

I was the first to protest. "All that in one day?" I whined.

"Mr. Jeffrey, you will please raise your hand if you have a question!" Mama retorted.

"But Mama," I continued, "I was planning to do some of my Christmas shopping this morn..."

"Mr. Jeffrey, I agreed for your cousins to come and spend Christmas with us in town ONLY if you all agreed to pull your weight and work quickly and efficiently. Calvin, Gregory, and Mikey, you all remember that?"

"Yes Mama/Aunty," they replied sheepishly. "Yes sir, Ma'am, Boss, Captain, Sergeant..."

Everyone burst out laughing. Everyone, except me. I sat down to read my long job description. "That's still too much," I complained again. But the others gave me such a ferocious "cut-eye" that I shut up immediately and dragged myself off to my first assignment. "I guess slavery is still legal in the West Indies," I moaned.

Mama heard me and said, "You want to leave early? Start early. Or get one or two of your "enslaved" friends in the neighbourhood to help you."

"But it's my Birthday," I answered mentally. "Nobody remembering that?" I tried to hold back the tears that were welling up in my eyes as I walked away.

It was Cousin Colette who asked the Million-Dollar Question. "And what is this Red Toothbrush at the bottom of the list?"

Mama did a double take, then said, "Oh, …am…that was just a slip. Not meant for you all at all. Look, sun up, so have your breakfast, and let's get going."

Then turning to Dad, she said, "Come Henry, we have our share to do!" Dad shook his head, smiled, and followed her into the house.

Mama told me later that as she walked off with Dad, she had a strong premonition that trouble was afoot.

As we were finishing breakfast, Gregory asked, "So, what is the real story behind the red toothbrush?"

"Christmas, for my mother," I answered, "means, among several other traditions, the purchasing of a new red toothbrush, usually from the Dominica Dispensary, and always in the last five minutes before the shops shut their doors. It is basically a superstition she got from her grandmother, and if she does not get that particular toothbrush, she believes that bad luck will follow her for the entire New Year."

"And you believe that too?" Calvin asked.

"Umm," I replied.

I smiled and moved off to begin my chores, my head dizzy in anticipation of the joys of Shopping Day. I could see myself in Roseau on Christmas Eve when the little city's commercial sector turned into an exciting playground filled with cars and trucks; children in their Sunday best taking home toys of all descriptions; and homemade sweets like coconut cheese, tablet haché, tamarind balls, and unbreakable (a hard peppermint delectable); apples and nougat. And how, when the shop lights came on at about 6 pm, the excitement went a pitch higher with kids running up and down with squeals of delight as they waved star-light sparklers and called out to each other; mothers warning them to look out for the bigger boys tossing mini bombs at passerby's feet; vendors hawking their merchandise; and a Santa or two whining their waist to some catchy Christmas calypso to the great amusement of everyone. It all ended at ten o'clock, when the shops closed their doors and shopkeepers and shoppers drifted off to their homes and churches for their Midnight Services. But I began to realise that this year I might not be part of that scene at all, given the number of assignments that lay before me.

At about eleven o'clock that morning, disaster struck. Mama was in the kitchen when Calvin shouted from upstairs "Ma? Ma? The lino for the passage is too short."

"Well, go back to the store and tell them to cut an extra piece for you. Is ten feet I told them not nine," said Ma.

"Been there, done that," said Gregory, Mikey and I together.

"They hadn't got more in that colour," said Mikey. "It finish."

"No more of the design or the colour?" asked Ma sensing another problem arising.

"Go and see for yourself," said Gregory.

"Look boy, don't be rude to me! I'm your Aunty!" Mama scolded.

"Sorry Aunty" he replied.

"Gregory, take this money and go by Red Store and see if they have it."

"Too late. It finish there too," Mikey and I said in unison.

"Go to your father and tell him what happen. He will know how to handle that problem," said Mama as she turned to speak with Zabet, the cook.

Upstairs in the drawing room, the girls were having no better luck. The two dried coconut husks used for polishing the floor were apparently too old for the kind of task they were being called upon to perform. They were falling apart in the girls' small but tough hands.

"And the Christmas tree fall down," chimed in Miss Fay.

"But nothing didn't break," Mara added.

"Well if you say so…" said Colette.

"Something break self!" said Fay. "The big star at the top. And all the lights stop lighting!"

"Not true!" said Mara.

"True!" said Fay.

"Not true!" said Mara.

"She lying!" said Fay.

"Who lying dere?" said Mara.

"OK. OK." Mama interjected. "The boys will fix it when they come back. Right now, I want to see everybody in the yard by the pond in ten seconds, starting now… Mikey where you going?"

"Nowhere," he replied.

"How you mean nowhere? I see you coming from under the mango tree where we boiling the ham," Mama said, growing more concerned with every second.

"Oh," said Mikey "I was just checking my bird."

"Bird? What bird?" Mama asked.

"Dis morning I put a bird to boil with de ham," he replied. "They say it will give each other flavour."

"What! You put it alive with all its feathers! Everything?" Mama shouted.

"Yes…, but it's dead now." Mikey replied.

"Dead now! Well your backside going and come alive when your uncle give you a few hot ones…" Mama screamed. "Everybody upstairs. I re-assigning all of you. But wait… where is Jeffrey?"

"He go and get Eugene to help us," Mikey replied.

"Wait, who you say?" Mama asked.

"Eugene," repeated Colette.

"Father in Heaven! Not Eugene!" Mama said with growing agitation.

"The mad boy from America?" asked Mara.

"Mad?" said Mama. "He more than mad. Last week he fall and roll down the front steps ten times, saying he is John Wayne dodging bullets in a saloon shoot out. And is only because he burst his mouth on the tenth time that he stop. I don't want him here again at all, at all," Mama said.

"Well, too late. Here he comes!" Calvin exclaimed.

All eyes immediately turn to the gate as we hear Eugene's voice shouting in a rank Brooklyn accent, "Come on, come in. Nobody gonna hurt you."

Eugene with three unknown boys march into the yard. "You see that dere? That's a pond. But for today this is the Río Grande because it is Christmas

Eve. Now first, I'm going to show you how John Wayne survives an Indian attack in the River Grande. I'm going to be John Wayne. Now let us see who's going to be the Indian Chief... OK you—the tall one—you're gonna be the Indian Chief. Pull out a gun and shoot me."

Out of nowhere, Mama comes running. "No, no, no. NO shooting. Nobody is going to be shot in this pond today."

"It is not a pond," says Eugene "It's the Río Grande."

"Whatever," says Mama.

But Tall Boy doesn't hear her. His hands go up slowly. "Bang," he says, pointing his finger like a gun. The other boys immediately join in, and the shooting frenzy ensues "Pow, Bang, Bang, Pow..."

Eugene turns around slowly, looks at the Indian Chief, puts up his hand to say something but the words don't come. He begins to tremble, his whole body shaking till he can stand no more. He freezes, his legs buckle under him, and he falls into the pond with a tremendous belly-splash, drenching everyone. A huge howl of admiration followed by hooting and clapping ensues. They look to the pond, but Eugene is nowhere to be seen in the pond's murky green waters. Twenty seconds go by, no Eugene. Thirty seconds, no Eugene. Thirty-five seconds, no Eugene.

Mama can't take no more. She jumps into the pond and searches around for Eugene. She finds him, pulls him up and jams him against the wall. "What on earth are you trying to do? Drive me crazy?" she screeches.

Eugene says, "Oh man! What you do dat for? Now you spoilt everything. I was just about to make my grand revival and end this battle by killing the Indian Chief and his men. Now I am going to have to start all over ag..."

"OH, NO. NO!" Mama shouted. "The director says cut! YOU are going to make a grand EXIT. Right now. All of you. OUT! The rest of you, upstairs! You are all in punishment. Nobody is going anywhere until shopping time at five o'clock."

"We?" says Gregory. "But we didn't do nothing."

"You clapped," Mama snapped. "You encouraged him. That's it. Everybody out!"

Eugene left quickly with his gang, we ran upstairs to wait for five o'clock, and Mama stood in the yard and sssscccreamed.

But that was not all for the afternoon. Just as Mama began mixing her cakes, there was a knock on the door. Mama answered it. It was Miss Johnson from the cathedral choir. "Mrs. B," she said. "Miss Evadney Richards say she cannot sing Minuit Chrétien tonight. She is leaving the church. And Mr. Francis Toulon has the flu, and he can hardly talk."

There was a long silence. Mama eventually asked, "So?"

"So, you will have to do it," said Miss Johnson.

"But it is in French," said Mama. "I don't know it in French."

"Neither does most of the congregation," whispered Miss Johnson with a sly little smile.

Both women looked to the sky, then Miss Johnson said, "Tell you what, we will type out the French version for you. You speak French Creole, don't you? Well, all you have to do is add some choice creole words in appropriate places and belt it loud on the chorus. I am sure that will work, don't worry. Rehearsal is from 2–3 pm. See you there. Bye." She turned quickly and disappeared down the street.

Mama sent Gregory to call her sister to take over the cake making while she went to the rehearsal. All the other traditions were observed including us children licking the bowl and spoon used to make the cake. However, some of the usual excitement was subdued as a result of the day's events.

Mama made it to work on time for her afternoon shift, and her employer even gave her time off to go and buy her traditional toothbrush fifteen minutes before closing time. But, alas, it was too late. There were no red toothbrushes left on the rack.

Mama was heartbroken. When she finally dragged herself home from work and recalled how her whole day was ruined, how badly the rehearsal had gone, and especially not having her red toothbrush for the first time since she had started the habit, she thought that she could just put her head in her hands and cry. Luckily for her, though, her cakes had just come back from Jake's Bakery and the house was full of the sweet aroma of hot Christmas cake. So, she got up, emptied two bottles of Sherry over the cakes, cut herself a huge slice from the biggest cake, and sat on the edge of her bed.

As she was about to eat it, I walked in. "Mama, you crying?" I asked.

"Yes," she said biting into a huge chunk of cake. "What else can I do? My whole day has been a total disaster, and I didn't even wish you Happy Birthday or let you know how proud we are of you. Here, have some cake." I bit into the warm cake, with its wine drenched fruits—oh that glorious taste of Christmas!

Mama continued, "Your father arranged a special gift for you. He hired the Union Club for your birthday party tomorrow, Christmas day. All your friends will be there. Lots of food, music and presents." I hugged her, and with tears streaming down our faces, we began laughing.

Mama had never been so early for church in all her life. By eleven fifteen she, Dad, and the seven children were taking a leisurely walk up Constitution Hill when a voice called to her, "Mrs. B can I have a word with you please." Of course, it was Eugene.

Mama sent us up the hill with Dad to wait for her and turned to him. "Yes Eugene, what is it now?"

Eugene approached her with an envelope and gift box. "This is for you, Mrs. B." Mama opened the envelope and read his crabby handwriting "Dear Mrs. B, I apologise for my behaviour this afternoon. Please accept this small token of my respect for you. Signed, Eugene."

She looked at the gift box. "Open it," said Eugene. Mama opened the box to find another long slender box inside. She opened the long box to find a red toothbrush encased in an airtight glass tube. Mama gasped.

"I found it at the bottom of the pond this afternoon. So, can we be friends?" asked Eugene. "My Grandma says I can come to church with you, if you agree."

Mama was in tears. She hugged him. "Yes, Yes," she said.

The children at the top of the hill cheered. Eugene took a bow, offered his right arm to Mama, who took it, and the group walked regally into the cathedral.

After church, a number of friends and family came over to congratulate Mama on her beautiful rendition of Minuit Chrétien, including her old French teacher, who told her that her diction was so clear that this was the first time he realised the shepherds were having agouti broth when the angels appeared. The whole room burst into laughter while Dad put on his favourite Christmas music, including "Drink your Rum on a Christmas Morning."

And so it was that the gifting of red toothbrushes as symbols of family love and unity (not to mention good hygiene) began and spread to all the towns and villages around the island. Of course, Mr. Eugene could not be outdone. Every year, he sends cartons of toothbrushes for Christmas to schools all over the world compliments Caribbean Stunts Inc., Hollywood,

California. Each box contains a sheet describing how he and I set up Mama's surprise gift that year. I am sure that you too would like to know how that was done, but that's a different story.

# Snake Woman

There were two distinct camps in my village: One which agreed with the head teacher that there were no such things as supernatural beings, except perhaps Papa God, who everyone knew was responsible for big events, such as life and death. Bush fires were more often than not caused by careless gardeners burning dry grass and twigs. Poor crops were the just reward of the lazy. Illness among livestock? Well, that could be easily explained with science and common sense, not obeah and magic, argued the head teacher and his followers.

Most of the inhabitants of my village, on the other hand, believed that supernatural creatures roamed the earth at night, wreaking havoc upon humans and animals alike. For instance, when Masie's six-month-old baby girl suddenly stopped eating, sleeping or growing and eventually died, the finger was pointed firmly at Ma Fanso, the notorious local witch, who everyone knew was the love rival of Masie's mum, now deceased. The two women had feuded bitterly for years and now it seemed Ma Fanso had finally avenged herself on her old enemy by stealing away the spirit of her only grand-child. That explained why all the children of the village would make a wide detour on their way to fetch water from the spring rather than walk through Ma Fanso's yard.

They were just as frightened of Mado, a young woman who all the grown-ups referred to as poor Mado. Far from being scary, I found Mado fascinating. In fact, when everyone else of my age group shunned her, I sought her company. On moonlit nights, when the

JANE ULYSSES GRELL is a retired teacher of French and English as an additional language. Published author, poet, storyteller and singer in the African-Caribbean oral tradition, she performs in schools, colleges, community groups and libraries in the UK and abroad. She works with BBC School Radio and is a frequent contributor to Scholastic Education's productions.

grown-ups entertained themselves with storytelling and the other children ran around playing ring games, I observed the stars under Mado's direction. She had her own names for the constellations and stories to accompany the names. She would say, "You see that likkle one there, the cross-eyed one that making sweet eyes at me? Well, is my grandmother Sousou who die before I was born."

"How you know that, Mado?" I would ask, listening attentively to her explanations which never varied. "I know is my grandmother. Since I born, she looking after me. Ma tell me that is why I so smart. I too clever for this village, you hear?"

Mado had a fine singing voice and used it, she said, to serenade the universe. She would stand for hours on end at the top of a secluded ridge over the White River, listening to and joining in with its "songs" as she called them. From time to time, she would make jottings in a dog-eared notepad. She told me in confidence that they were her little secrets, hers and the river's. With much running up and down scales, deep breathing and stretching, she never tired of warbling her harmonies to the accompaniment of the river's gurgling. The echoes sometimes wafted over the village on lazy breezes. At such times, people would shake their heads sadly and say, "The thing taking Mado again, poor petit." In their minds she always remained the "poor little one," even after she had grown into a quite rotund woman.

The older people who knew her as a child said Mado used to be a remarkably clever pupil at school; clever enough to win a scholarship to attend high school. But it was not to be. The head teacher had in fact entered her for the common entrance examinations. However, the night before she was due to make the ten-mile journey to sit the exam in Roseau, Mado fell ill with a burning fever. She tossed and turned and did battle with all manner of wild beasts trying to pluck at her eyes. It took her days to recover from her delirium, and since then, they swore "Poor Mado never been de same again."

During her illness, every member of the village who could walk had filed past the open doorway of Mado's house, ostensibly to offer words of comfort to her parents. Of course, they really came only to stare at the sick girl lying on the sofa of their tiny living room. The gossip mongers had a field day, competing with one another for the most compelling blow by blow account of what they claimed they saw and heard.

"Well, from what I see," exclaimed Mrs Norris, "is as if de chile was possess by a spirit. One minute she opening her mouth wide, wide and letting out one set of bawling, next minute she opening and closing her mouth like a fish, but nothing coming out."

Ma Joe added, "An you din see her hands? De chile fingers turn to claws. They had to tie them so she wouldn't tear up her own face."

"Well, what I see, and I not lying," confided Ferdy the antiman in a lowered voice. "The girl belly was going up and down, up and down. You coulda swear it was a ti bolom dancing inside the poor chile. Lord, have mercy." And he made the sign of the cross.

After two days of this shameless exhibition, Mado's dad had finally had enough. He shouted at all passersby to stop using his yard as a public road and to leave his daughter in peace. He glared and wildly brandished a sharp cutlass.


On the third morning, they were preparing to take her in a hammock for the long and treacherous foot journey into town, where she could be seen by a doctor, when the fever broke. Mado called for a glass of water and something to eat, then fell into a long, deep sleep.

The girl who emerged from her illness was a very different creature from the one known to the village. She now inhabited a strange and distant world from which her family and everyone else were shut out. Going to school was out of the question. Mado now woke up at all hours, shouting the house down. Often, she wandered off in the dead of night to no one knew where. Her church attendance ceased after the priest, at the request of her parents, conducted an exorcism to drive away what they were sure were evil spirits. When people left her alone, Mado would sometimes be drawn by the organ music and the singing of the choir to listen from outside the church, joining in at full throttle.

At first, children would follow her around, mocking and chanting. "Mad Mado; mad, mad maddy Mado!" But as their taunts fell on deaf ears, they soon tired of their sport and Mado was left free to wander the length and breadth of the village.

As she grew older, Mado's peculiarities increased or, by the head teacher's reckoning, Mado's mental condition worsened. "That's what you get when you live in a place behind God's back, with no doctors for medical care, and nothing but superstition," he complained bitterly. "I know someone just like poor Magdalene who was sent to Barbados for treatment and came back completely cured. Not only was he able to complete his studies, he is right now a high up in the police force."

But none of the arguments made any difference to Mado's chaotic existence. By day she mostly slept—sometimes at home, but more often than not, in the shade of a tree. She favoured the beautiful flamboyant tree standing in a shallow gully near the village cross roads. She told me once that invisible magical creatures often came to dance and taylaylay under that tree, with its spreading branches and profusion of bright orange flowers. They always invited her to join them. By night, she wandered the village and could occasionally be heard honing her vocal techniques from the river bank.

Her parents and people from the village became seriously worried when Mado took to sitting for hours on a large rock in the middle of the river. Come rain or shine she just sat on that stone and performed with her imaginary orchestra. Her parents came to accept that there were no locks strong enough to keep her from this latest hideout and decided to let her be. Well, that river was treacherous. With its source high up in the mountains, not far from the boiling lake, the White River could swell to bursting and advance without warning—a swift, brown bulldozer, sweeping away anything and everything in its path.

One evening in early June, at the start of the hurricane season, the heavens opened and strong gusts lashed out, twisting branches and breaking off the tops of tall coconut and breadfruit trees.

Both parents agreed. "We cannot let Mado stay out there tonight, non." So together, they took a hurricane lamp and headed for the large rock in the river, but to their dismay, she wasn't there. They called out several times, scouring the banks of the river for as long as they could. "The river wash her away," her mother said, weeping.

"But we don't know that," said the dad. "Mado too smart to let river take her, just like that. She O.K., I tell you."

They returned home to sound the alarm, whereupon neighbours and half the village came to help with the search, but to no avail. The search was called off when it seemed too dangerous to be out and about, given the impenetrable darkness, howling winds and relentless rain, not to mention the unstoppable swelling of the river. They resumed at first light, by which time the gale had subsided and morning tip-toed out with the clean, rain-washed calm which comes after a storm. Someone suggested that it might be a good idea to revisit her old haunt, and, sure enough, there sat Mado on her rock in the river, glaring fiercely at the band of intruders.

I think that was the moment when Mado withdrew completely from the village, though she continued to communicate with me. I didn't appreciate at the time the importance of my interpreter role. After she had beckoned to me, I had to be carried on her dad's shoulder as he waded almost to his chest through the strong current. When he had placed me safely on the stone and waded back to join the others, Mado whispered in my ear.

Immediately, everyone wanted to know, "What she saying?"

"She say she want something to eat." I called out across the water. "And she say she want her clothes and some bedding and after that, you must leave her alone to get on with her life."

Normally, people laughed at the strange things which Mado said and did, but not on that day. Instead, a kind of heaviness descended on the people of the village. Mado's mum cried quietly while her father looked on helplessly.

"What she mean, leave her to get on with her life?" said a neighbour.

"What life, non?" another neighbour cheupsed loudly.

Suggestions flew around. "You need to bring de priest to take away the spell from your daughter. She have a demon in her."

Another neighbour went too far as she addressed the parents. "All you too soft with that girl, you hear. She spoilt. All you always let her do what she want, since she small. Now, look how she turn out." That was Effel. She was notorious for letting her big mouth run away with her, so no one paid her any mind.

From that day onwards, random items of food were left on the river bank for Mado. My mother, though wary at first, took a certain pride in the fact that Mado trusted me even above her own parents, so she allowed me to visit her, provided I kept to the relative safety of the river bank. One day, when I got to the river, bearing food and clean bedding, there was no sign of Mado on her rock. I then heard footsteps behind me and she beckoned me to follow her. "I want to show you my house and my family," she said conspiratorially before disappearing into a cave whose narrow entrance was hidden by wild ferns and vine creepers.

I was mystified and apprehensive, but curiosity got the better of me. I followed her into the cave which was just wide enough to accommodate an adult. It was under a large overhanging rock with many ridges and crevices. She used the ridges as shelves to store an assortment of shells and pebbles, seeds and pods, shrubs and wild flowers. The crevices were blocked with dry grass and banana leaves, to keep out the draught, she explained. The floor was firm and dry but there was a damp, musty smell about the place and something else too, which I couldn't quite put my finger on. She saw the bewildered look on my face and said with a satisfied grin. "I have another room, you know."

"Another room?" I echoed stupidly.

"Yes, where my family live."

"Your family?" I was beginning to sound like a parrot.

"Well, only the daddy. Some nasty boys threw stones at the mother and the babies and kill them. But I save Jeffrey."

I had no idea who Jeffrey was, but I had a feeling I didn't really want to know. I started backing out of the cave entrance.

"Is alright. Jeffrey is beautiful," said Mado, shuffling off to a small side cave and returning with a huge boa constrictor wrapped around her waist and shoulders. I screamed and bolted towards the exit.

"Jeffrey won hurt you. He's my friend," I heard her say from yards away. I fled without saying goodbye. If the village knew that Mado shared her living space with a giant snake, I had no idea what they would think or do. I know it would break her mother's heart, kill her from worry and shame. Yet Mado seemed happy. But was she safe? How long could she go on living in a cave with a snake? I felt that I couldn't tell anyone as this was Mado's secret.

That night, I slept very badly, twisting and turning. I found myself engulfed in a pit full of writhing boa constrictors. I woke up screaming. In my dream I had visited Mado's cave to bring her usual supplies. I was greeted by a large snake swaying from the branch of a gommier tree. He said in a slow, hypnotic voice, "Mado was my ole name. My new name is Snake Woman. Go an tell dem. Snake Woman is my name now, you hear me?" Then the creature broke into a low, raucous laugh that turned my skin into goose bumps.

My mother woke me up. She bent over me and mopped the beads of perspiration trickling down my brow. I was burning with a fever. She kept me from school that day, saying, "There's a nasty bug going round. You better stay home for today and I'll make you some strong bush tea. It will drive the fever away. You have your common entrance examination coming soon. You cannot afford to fall sick. Stay in bed and rest yourself, dou-dou. Poor petit."

Relieved, I lay back gratefully and closed my eyes. But no matter how hard I tried, I could not drive away the haunting image of Mado, the Snake Woman.

# Affiliation

The interview was going so well, I made the mistake of allowing myself to hope. The manager scanned my certificates and I held my breath. I'd done well in my year, five ones and two twos, and A levels in maths and political science. Plus, he didn't know me personally. He was from Antigua. There was still a chance.

"Well young man, these look very promising," he smiled at me over his bifocals. I exhaled and gave a lopsided smile in return. I wiped the sweat off my palms onto my slacks. He scanned the questionnaire I'd been required to fill, and then he frowned. Dread began to twist in my stomach.

He looked at me quizzically.

"You forgot to tick off under political affiliation, son." He pushed the form across the table at me. I knew it was useless, but I felt the words tumble out of my mouth.

"I don't have one. I'm neutral. I don't have an interest in politics," I babbled. He stared at me, and his bushy eyebrows rose slowly.

"So you don't support the current administration?" His tone became stern. I tried to meet his gaze but I felt so disarmed, I couldn't.

I licked my dry lips. I couldn't fail. Not again. *Just tell him what he wants to hear*, I thought.

"I don't vote. I don't believe in partisan politics," I said. I heard the hopeless tone in my voice.

"Well that's...naïve. So you must be a supporter of the opposition then." He pulled the form towards him,

NICOLE GEORGES-BENNETT is a Dominican freelance journalist, Christian wife and mother, residing in Toronto, Canada. She enjoys writing sci-fi and fantasy and has written the novel *Tales of St. Marts*. Additionally, Nicole is the script writer for the radio program "*Redemption Road*" and worked on the anthology *The Flying Crapaud*, published in 2020.

opened a desk drawer and dropped it in. He carefully put my certificates back into their folder and handed them to me. I took them automatically.

"I don't support any party," I repeated, "I believe Government should work for the good of all citizens, regardless of party affiliation." At that moment the door opened and his secretary came in. My heart sank. She had not been at her desk when I came in an hour earlier, so I'd escaped her sharp gaze. She was from my neighbourhood, and she knew me. It was over.

I stood up and stuck out my hand stiffly to him. The manager glanced at it dubiously and then shook it. I turned and I saw the shock of recognition on his secretary's face. As I left, I closed the door but not before I heard her scandalised whisper, "His head not good, you know. He was in Psychiatric unit after his father die."

I walked quickly, and wiped away hot tears from the corners of my eyes. I could have done that job blindfolded if he'd just given me a chance. I would have been the best employee he'd ever had. I caught the bus home and stripped off; I had soaked through my dress shirt and jacket. I did my breathing exercises and I repeated my mantra: *I am well. All is well. All shall be well.* I could hear the whispering of voices at the edge of my consciousness trying to break through, so I built my mental wall, brick by brick. By the time I was finished, I was exhausted but proud. I had not let the voices win.

My mother came home during her lunch hour, and we ate sancoche with dumplings. She chewed methodically, but I could feel her eyes boring into my skull.

"So you open your big mouf and you doh get de job, not true?" She scraped her fork back and forth over the plate loudly. I glanced up and saw her wipe her face with tissue, leaving wisps of white fluff in the creases of her eyes and in the folds of her neck. She got up and pulled my plate from me. I had saved a last dumpling, and I watched glumly as she put the whole thing in her mouth. She dropped the plates with a clatter in the sink.

"All you have to say is I voting MPP or PPM. That's all you have to say. You stubborn just like your father," she said from between clenched teeth. I watched her shoulders heave, and I could feel the voices pressing against my mental wall.

"I can't do that, Mammy. Nobody should be forced to support a political party just to get basic human rights and necessities," I said.

*Keep calm. Don't get angry. All is well.*

"Boy, you are twenty-three years-old. You doh have job, you doh have house, you doh even have a woman. You crazy in your head, and you need expensive medicine. I cannot take all that burden!"

She rounded on me holding a spoon and pointed it at me as her voice rose.

"How you think you getting de little food we have? How you think you get money to go school in foreign? Your father with his big talk about democracy! He could never get a job, or buy land... couldn't even get a place to rent because his mouf never stop running! Is me that had to go beg the minister to send you school. You think that was easy for me to do? Ah?" She jabbed the spoon at me, and I felt each jab like a knife stab, tearing through my fragile psyche.

"He was a man of integrity," I said. "He believed in a free and fair democracy. He spoke out against this oppressive system." I saw the anger in her eyes become a deep, dark sadness.

"He die like a dog in his own vomit because no doctor in town would take him," she said. "When he was so sick that last time, we sit in the E.R. in the hallway and those nurse walk up and down by us. Nobody doh check us. The minute I say his name, the Matron say his voter card show he doesn't vote, and he not a true patriot."

Sorrow rose out of her and surrounded her like a black storm cloud. It looked like she was drowning in it.

I started to open my mouth to warn her, but suddenly realised it might be better not to.

"You taking your pills, nah?" she asked. Her eyes narrowed suspiciously.

I nodded because I couldn't trust myself to lie. I tried not to, but I began to picture my father lying on the floor of a hospital hallway. I knew I shouldn't think like that. It was a dangerous train of thought.

In my imagination, he lay on the cold floor. Was it tiled or bare concrete? Did he feel the cold seep into his fevered bones? I looked through his eyes at the stockinged feet and orthopedic shoes flashing by. Did he regret his obsession for equality? All he had to do was say the right words, declare his party, announce his colours, or wave a flag to save his life. But he didn't. Instead, *he died like a dog* as my mother had described it.

I felt fury build up in me. Not at the way of life that dictated I must align politically in order to get food, shelter and education. I was angry at my father for his outlandish principles and stubborn refusal to conform.

The voices echoed so loudly in my head that they shattered the protective wall I had so carefully constructed. They ran rampant into every corner of my mind.

*I am well. All is well. All shall be well.*

But voices screamed louder and gave me a new mantra.

*He was a fool. You are a fool. You will die like a fool.*

My mother, her head and torso the only things visible from the storm cloud only I could see, left the house to go back to work. I went to the sink and started to wash up, but the gleam of the silver knives seduced me. I rinsed the soap off my shaking hands and went to my room. I had two doses left in the bottle my mother had begged from a nurse at the public clinic. Because of my father, she would never have clear access to the necessities of life, but because she attended a political party's campaign meetings, she managed to eke out a living as a public toilet cleaner.

I would never be so lucky. I had inherited my father's disease—a conscience that could not be compromised.

River Ridge Press, Dominica Prize for Romance goes to Kathy MacLean for *Un Ti Bo*. "This charming short story recalls a time of innocence when the ideals of etiquette, ethics, and young love were as fresh as the island's trade winds. Despite the hurdles of race and class, our hero exercises patience and perseverance as he reaches for the gold ring of his dreams."

# Un Ti Bo

KATHY MACLEAN lives in London but has strong ties with Dominica where she was born. She spent her teenage years in Ethiopia. Her writings on children's literacy and primary education have been published in academic journals, books and a co-authored educational pack linking Dominican and British history. *Un Ti Bo* is her first work of fiction.

I first noticed her one afternoon when the *Bwa Caribe* was in full bloom, as she walked through the Botanic Gardens with her companions. I was sitting in the shade of the broad branched banyan tree reading *Great Expectations*. Except for the bird song and the thud of fruit falling from the nearby cannonball tree, it was a dreamy, peaceful afternoon. Occasionally I would lift my eyes to take in the beauty of the palms and the plants which formed the view around me. This was a favourite refuge of mine.

The sound of laughter and high girlish voices drew me away from Pip's agonising about Estella. I looked up and saw a group of three young women talking animatedly. I knew that they must be from one of the Roseau Creole families; all three were pale skinned, but the shortest of the three sported a hint of gold, the warm tones of the *mulâtresse*. I noticed her luxuriant dark hair escaping her hat and the eyes which appeared too large for her almond-shaped face. She was recounting some incident which seemed to throw her companions into paroxysms of laughter. She glanced in my direction, and for a moment the tamarind eyes met mine. My heart skipped a beat and then began a dance of its own. However, I believe that I remained invisible in the shade of the great tree.

Who was she? I wanted to know more. I was captivated by this '*ti belle fi*'. How could I find out? From her dress and manner, I knew that I would not find her wandering around the market square or strolling through the port. As the young women moved on, I noticed that they were being followed by two older women walking at a more leisurely pace and carrying umbrellas against the sun.

The taller of the two called out, 'Girls, slow down! This is supposed to be a pleasant afternoon stroll! *Les jeunes sont toujours pressé,*' she complained to her companion.

'*Eh bien*, you'd think they were carrying an urgent message,' replied the other.

I smiled at the impatience of age and youth. Luckily, I knew the older women. They were the Gillet sisters, chaperoning their nieces, which was good and bad. Good, because I would be able to track her down, but bad because it was well-known that Mamselle Marie Claire and Mamselle Juliette, the chaperones, were snobs who did not believe in the mixing of the races or classes. They took a great pride in their French heritage, their soft silken tresses and pale skin. I had heard that they were horrified when their brother Jean had fallen for '*une femme negre*'.

As I watched the women disappear through an avenue of mahogany trees, I resolved to find out more. I could not return to my book. My concentration had vanished along with their gay laughter and skipping feet. The world around me seemed different; it was not and would never be the same again. I realised that I was humming '*If you were the only girl...*' and the tune lifted me as music always does.

On the way home, I visited my friend Louis and his wife Francine. We sat on the veranda with its view towards the Roseau harbour, chatting over a glass of rum. The warm evening breeze ruffled the leaves of the fruit trees in their garden. The sun was beginning its descent into the sea transforming it to a burnt ochre.

'You seem distracted tonight,' Francine remarked, '*Un ti bazoudi!*'

Louis laughed. 'He saw a girl. You know, one of the Gillets. The one called Angela, *la petite mulâtresse*. She seems to have taken his mind with her.'

'I see,' Francine mused. 'Well, Joe. You always were a man for a challenge, *non! Bon chance.*'

I knew she was right; it would be a challenge. Who was going to introduce me in the first place? We did not move in the same circles. I was still regarded by some as just another boy from the country who was trying to make his way in the city. Anyway, why would a girl like that even notice me?

The next time I saw her, it was on the Sunday of that week, and I was in the church choir stalls. I had placed my music for the mass on the stand and was looking down into the congregation at the throng of arrivals, gay in their

Sunday finery. The older women wore darker colours, while the young were dressed in brilliant bird of paradise garments, their hats adorned with plumes and flowers. Some wore tied heads, *tête mawé* of bright madras, and *Wòb Dwiyet*. The men in their suits or shirts and ties lent a more sombre note. The older ladies walked in leaning on their canes, brandishing bamboo fans against the rising heat as they took their seats.

Suddenly there she was. Angela! I would have known that head with the dark curls under the hat trimmed with blue anywhere. A slight figure with white gloved hands, a small piece of pale sky against the vibrant colours. She was with a dark-skinned woman dressed in the *Grand Wòb*, resplendent in a flamboyant of red and gold. Just before entering their pew, Angela stopped and looked up into the choir stall. I gazed into her dark eyes and held them for a moment. I smiled and I swear that she smiled back!

I could hardly breathe. I bowed my head, and humming the *Agnus Dei*, tried to compose myself. Perhaps the light-headed feeling and the fluttering between my ribs was because I had not yet eaten that day.

A hush fell as the priest and acolytes entered in procession. The choir master lifted his baton. The organ sprang into life and we raised our voices in the *Asperges Me*. As I sang and our voices climbed into the flying buttresses and beyond, my soul soared and became the song. Just then, all that mattered was the music.

At the end of the service, I saw her again, standing at the foot of the steps with the woman I believed was her mother. I removed my hat and bowed courteously in their direction. Her mother acknowledged me with a stiff nod of her head. As I turned away, I noticed that among the people who walked over to greet them was my employer, Mr. Rose. Perhaps he would put in a good word!

I was working as a legal clerk to one of the foremost lawyers in our island. I hoped that some of his local standing and prestige would reflect on me and thereby enhance my reputation. I sauntered off to meet my own family, humming under my breath.

The rest of the day was spent with friends. We walked to the Roseau River carrying our bath towels. Someone had a bottle of rum, one of the girls had the lime squash. I had persuaded my mother to part with some bakes, which we had filled with saltfish. This and the mangoes we were carrying would make a very pleasant picnic, although Cecil kept moaning that someone had forgotten the bitters.

Our afternoon was spent swimming and jumping off the huge rocks, seeing who could make the biggest splash.

The next day, I was sitting at my desk carefully writing out the documents outlining the purchase of a plot of land in Newtown when I was summoned by my boss. I walked into his book-lined office wondering what additional task he had in mind for me, or if he had heard about how rowdy we had been on the way home from the river, after a few rum punches.

'I believe you've got some teaching experience, haven't you?' he asked. 'Would you be interested in doing some private tuition?'

'Well, yes, I suppose. But who wants it?'

'Mrs Gillet is looking for someone to help her daughter Angela with her French. I mentioned that you might do it. I know you have a knowledge of that language. After all you have been able to communicate with our clients in Guadeloupe and Martinique very successfully.'

I returned to my desk floating on air. I could not believe my luck. I now had a chance to meet the girl whose face had haunted me for the past week. The afternoon passed in a daze. At the end of the day, I visited Louis and Francine to share this news with them.

As I was leaving, Francine cautioned, '*Pwan garde, lanmè pa ni bwanch!*'

I knew she was right; I could get caught up in a situation which I could not control.

A few days later the arrangements were made, and I set off. Was this a stroke of luck, or would I be put in a position which would make things worse? Well, I would get to meet Angela, at least. My mouth was dry, and my hands were sweaty. I felt ungainly, my feet were too big, my head was too small.

On reaching the house in Roseau, I was shown up the stairs, where I was greeted by Mme Gillet. I bowed towards her and put out my right hand. She did not offer hers. I said hoarsely, 'My name is Joseph Raphael. My employer Mr Rose said that you needed a tutor for your daughter.'

She invited me into the drawing room. It was already occupied by Angela's aunts. They offered me a seat in a straight-backed chair. The three ladies then proceeded to interview me. I expected them to ask me questions about my experience and qualifications. But no, they wanted to know who my parents were and if they were married. Did I attend mass regularly? Who were my friends? Did I drink? It was all rather bizarre, but I must have given the right answers because at the end of the grilling, I was told that I could start the next week.

A few days later, I overheard something very troubling. Mr Sandford, a well-known businessman, came into the office to meet my employer. I was asked to fetch them some refreshments. As I entered the room to serve the drinks, Sandford was rubbing his hands in delight as he said, 'Well, we are about to take the properties in Roseau. We just have to get to Soufriere tomorrow, and we will be able to seize the houses there and the estates. I mean the man has no business sense—it's all in his name! I don't think that he can have read the conditions, he will think that he still has time to pay up, and he will default on the loan. And that will be one in the eye for that pompous Jean Gillet and his family. The wife is his sister you know.'

I glanced at the papers on the desk and recognised the name of the person he was referring to. I had met the gentleman; these were kind and trusting people. I could see that they were now going to be destitute. It had been rumoured before that this particular businessman, Sandford, was into some sharp practice. I was surprised that Mr Rose appeared to condone it.

I returned to my desk to attend to the papers I was working on. I found it difficult to concentrate as the knowledge I now possessed troubled me. It seemed wrong to me and I felt that a trick was being played out. The air was still, and the room seemed closer, stifling despite the open window. I gazed out of the window at the cloudless sky and an idea began to form. Perhaps there was something I could do.

I gathered some papers together and left the office as quickly as was reasonable. I hastened to the jetty where I found some fishermen about to sail south. They agreed to give me passage. Later that afternoon, we sailed into Soufrière Bay and landed opposite the church framed by wind-blown coconut palms. I disembarked and was given directions to the home of the Oliviers.

On arriving, I introduced myself and explained the reason for my visit. M. Olivier put his head in his hands and sighed. 'Such wickedness! I was warned not to go into business with that man.'

Mme. Olivier asked if nothing could be done. It was then that I explained my plan. The priest and local registrar were sent for and between us we drew up the papers to transfer all the houses and estates owned by M. Olivier to Mme. Olivier. Early next morning, the fishermen transported me back to Roseau. I wish that I had been able to witness the disappointment of the bailiffs when they arrived to collect their pound of flesh.

I suppose I was fortunate that news of my intervention did not get back to my employer, but I hated injustice and felt triumphant at my small victory

This was perhaps the longest week of my life. The days crawled. I wandered through the gardens hoping that I would come across Angela and her aunts on one of their walks. I persuaded some friends to join me to play a game of cricket on the pitch. However, I was so distracted that it annoyed my team-mates.

I caught sight of her again at mass on Sunday, I watched her from the choir stalls and hoped to have an opportunity to greet her at the end of the service. But Father Labat asked us to stay on after the service to discuss singing at a wedding on the next Saturday.

So, on the following Wednesday, I began tutoring Angela Gillet under the fierce gaze of either her mother or one of her aunts.

As the weeks went by, they began to accept my presence more readily, and we would at times find ourselves alone. At the end of one of my visits, Mamselle Juliette took me aside, and I wondered what I'd done.

'My sister told us how you helped them. Thank you.' I opened my mouth to respond but she had already turned away. It was never referred to again, but on my next visit, one of the maids brought in a pot of tea and some biscuits.

During the periods of practising conversation in French, I tried to find out something about her life. I soon knew that she enjoyed reading romances, drawing and embroidery. She also seemed fascinated by magic and the spirit world. On one occasion, she asked me if I had heard about the soucouyant in Mahaut and told me about the old woman who had come to market from a country village and refused to walk on the right side of the road.

After this discussion, I leant her my copy of *Wuthering Heights*, and she became intrigued with Heathcliff and Catherine, who seemed to ignite her imagination.

I discovered that she had two older brothers. One of them was living with family in Martinique, and the other had gone to Cuba. 'They have gone to seek their fortune.' She laughed with her eyes crinkling at the edges. 'My father says they have to try to make their way in life. I'm a girl, so I'm excused.' This seemed to amuse her even more.

During one of our sessions, she was very excited to tell me that she was going with her parents to visit her family in Soufriere that weekend. 'We are to stay with Tanty Elise and her family. We will take the launch on Friday to Soufriere, and on Saturday will go to their house on Morne Acouma for a few days. I love it there! They have lots of open space and horses. I love exploring and being on High Meadow. The view is just incredible.' I asked her to repeat that in French. Which she did. Then she said much more quietly. 'My parents were talking about you last night.'

I looked at her inquiringly, and she continued. 'Did you know that the Oliviers at Soufrière are our close relatives? Mme. Olivier is my Tanty Elise, my father's sister. Papa said that you saved them from ruin. He also said it was a secret and that you were a brave man.'

I could feel myself flushing under her earnest gaze and said rather abruptly that we needed to concentrate on the text that we had been reading. I knew how important it was to be acknowledged and noticed by these people.

Angela already had a good basic knowledge of the French language. She was quick to learn, and after some weeks, I took pleasure in introducing her to the poetry of Daniel Thaly, a poet of Martinique and Dominica.

I tried to be professional, but I would catch myself gazing at her as she bent over her books. I had to steady myself when she looked at me through those questioning eyes. One evening as we read *Clair de la Lune à Minuit* together, the sibilant sounds of the poem caressed our ears. Our hands touched just for a moment, and Angela slipped her fingers into mine. A fire burned my cheeks, and the refrain of a folk song burst into my head; 'Ba mwen un ti bo!' If she only knew what I was thinking! 'Give me a little kiss…'

When I left that evening, I could still feel the softness of her fingers. Under the bright moon, carried along by a tide of hope and promise, I whistled, '*Ba Mwen Un Ti Bo*' all the way home.

# Jorgee

The weather had hastened the dusk to night, and the savannah was a pool of mud. Head bent and bare feet, Jorgee trudged across the field while trying to maintain his balance. It hurt in places where the boys had kicked him. He looked up briefly, but couldn't see his house in the distance—the torrential rain, tears and lack of glasses blurred his vision. Jorgee's clothes stuck to his body despite the plastic poncho his mother had made him. He hated wearing those things. The Jenson brothers said his long limbs stuck out from them like a scarecrow. His stomach growled and he thought about the bakes and cacao with bay leaf and spice his mother, Pauline, had promised to make. He hoped it would be ready when he got home.

A flash illuminated the heavens and the deafening crash that followed made Jorgee yelp. He lost his footing and the grip on his schoolbag loosened. Sitting in the mud, cold and in pain, he wiped his eyes on the wet poncho with the crook of his elbows. He stood after a few attempts and stretched out his hands trying to get them clean as he walked. When Jorgee finally made it across the savannah, the poncho was torn, and his feet were aching. He struggled up the slippery path to his house, relying on the overgrown plants for support.

The house was in darkness. Calling out to his mother, Jorgee wearily climbed the five concrete steps that led to the front door. It was a wooden Dutch door, the type where the bottom half could remain shut, while the top half was open. He banged on it just as another flash of lightning lit the sky.

LISA J. LATOUCHE is a published writer from Dominica. She's a graduate of the University of Leicester and a former Writer in Residence at the UWI St. Augustine Campus. Presently, she's pursuing her MFA in Creative Writing at the University of Maryland and working on two novels.

"Mammy!" The booming thunder rattled the wooden house. "Open de door!"

Rain pelted his body like little darts where the thin poncho didn't cover. Jorgee looked back at the savannah. The large trees surrounding the flat land looked ominous. He pounded furiously on the door, slowly realising that every knock was futile. Frustration swept over him as he dejectedly sank to the step. Where was his mother?

Jorgee could hear his heartbeat like a loud, off beat drum. He contemplated going into the cellar but was afraid there might be rats or other crawling animals down there. He decided to brave the darkness and walk to the back of the house to the bedroom he shared with his mother. Maybe she had fallen asleep. It was unlike her to go out in the evenings. By that time, the torrential showers had ceased leaving in their wake a light rain. He held out his hands to keep his balance. Once at the back, Jorgee climbed the few steps and pounded on the rear door. "Mammy?" Hearing no answer, he bent to look through the gap in the bottom part of the door. Usually, he could see the foot of his mother's bed from that vantage point. Now, he saw nothing. She must have blocked it with a cloth. Jorgee returned to the front and craned his neck to see if there was light in the neighbour's house further up the hill. He wanted to go there but was afraid the woman who lived there might be a *soukouyan* like people said. He remained on the steps, gripped by uncertainty and fear.

Jorgee had made up his mind to tell his mother about the Jenson brothers, her boss's sons. She had been the Jensen's housekeeper for as long as Jorgee could remember. He didn't want to cause any trouble, but the bullying was getting worse. Mrs. Jenson was an eye doctor and Mr. Jenson was an important man in government. Jorgee knew the boys bullied him because of his stupid name. He knew if he had a father, nobody would tease him. As a matter of fact, a father would have never named him Jorgee. *Georgie Porgie pudding and pie.* He hated the stupid rhyme, and he hated his stupid name.

Jorgee felt someone shaking him. His entire body ached and he fought to get air into his lungs. He opened his eyes slightly then shut them, fighting off the glare from a lamp.

"Jorgee." It was his mother's gentle voice.

"*By dose* block," Jorgee wheezed. His congestion affected his speech. His chest heaved in discomfort, and he coughed uncontrollably.

His mother was sitting in a chair next to him wearing an oversized t-shirt and dabbing his bruises with rubbing alcohol. Her head was tied in a forest green scarf, and there were creases of worry across her forehead. Her eyebrows furrowed, and instead of the twinkle in her brown eyes, he saw an expression of concern. The lamp cast a glow on her dark skin forcing the hollow of her cheeks to appear deeper. Her small mouth curved downward.

"You want some water?" She stood, thin yet strong.

Jorgee nodded. He was wearing a clean t-shirt and propped up against yellow pillows on his mother's bed. The mattress he normally slept on was leaning against the wooden wall, away from the buckets that were catching errant raindrops from their rusty corrugated zinc roof. Mr. Jenson had promised to replace their roof and add a room for Jorgee since the last election four years ago but hadn't kept his promise.

His mother handed him the water and felt his forehead with the back of her hand. Jorgee sipped a little from the plastic cup and gave it back to her.

"How—I—reach?" he asked in between coughs.

"You passed out on the step and I carried you inside," Pauline said. "Here's some pumpkin soup." Jorgee shook his head in protest but his mother insisted. As she spoon-fed him, she asked him where he had been and what had happened. He opened his mouth to speak, but tears rolled down his cheeks instead of words leaving his mouth. His mother held him gently and stroked his head as he fought to breathe. Jorgee could feel the bone between her small breasts. Her hands were calloused but comforting.

"We'll talk about it later," she said. "The ambulance coming to take us to the hospital."

Not long after, Pauline covered Jorgee with a thick blanket. The paramedic carried him down the hill and across the savannah on his back, while she held a flashlight to guide them. The sky had already cleared.


Jorgee was wheeled to the Children's Ward. It was dimly lit, painted light blue, smelling of medication and disinfectant. Most of the children were asleep. Jorgee's grey metal cot was flanked by a tall green oxygen tank and a small metal table. On the opposite side of the room was a pretty Kalinago girl he had seen in the Emergency Room, while enduring three rounds of nebuliser. She was buried under a yellow sheet and only her long black hair was visible. A radio was playing somewhere and the nurses' voices found their way to Jorgee's ears. He already longed for the quiet of his home.

His mother was on her cell phone at the foot of his bed talking to Mr. Jenson, her boss, telling him that Jorgee had caught a pneumonia and that she would be late for work. A fit of coughing overtook Jorgee, leaving him weak and breathless. A nurse hurried to his side and placed a small tube just under his nostrils.

"Some oxygen will make you feel better, sweetie," the nurse assured him as she checked her watch. Her complexion was dark chocolate as were her eyes. After she left, Pauline rubbed his forehead, between his brows to his hairline— up and down, up and down. He'd always liked how that felt.

"How you feeling now?" she asked.

"Sleepy," he wheezed.

"You'll feel better in a few days."

Jorgee nodded and closed his eyes. The hum of the ward seemed loud. Machines. Voices. He asked his mother why she wasn't at home when he got there.

"I didn't see you coming, so I go and look for you. Now I need to know what happen."

"Kalid *ad* Krisan beat be up. They take *by* shoes. Lose *by* glasses."

He heard his mother gasp. She stopped rubbing. "Jenson children hit you? And they take back the shoes?"

He hadn't known the shoes were hand-me-downs, but he wasn't surprised.

"I pay plenty money for that glasses, Jorgee."

"They always troubling *be* at school."

"How comes you never tell me that?"

Jorgee sighed. He'd wanted to, but he didn't want to cause problems between his mother and her employer. Another bout of coughing racked him. His mother adjusted his pillows. "You going to be twelve soon, you have to learn to defend yourself. And you mustn't keep things from me." Jorgee nodded as tears dropped from his eyelids.

"I slaving for Jenson children and they abusing you like that!" She sucked her teeth. "I will let their father deal with them."

"So what about *by* father?" Jorgee looked at his mother. "I want *hib* to deal with *theb* too."

Pauline took a deep breath and looked away.

Jorgee thought about comments Kalid had made about their grandfather, Lawyer Jenson, being Jorgee's father. He was aware of his uncanny resemblance to the man and wondered if this pleasant, generous lawyer was truly his father. This man, who always gifted him at birthdays and Christmas.

"We'll talk about it another time. Try to sleep." Pauline resumed the gentle massage of the space between his eyebrows.


On his fifth day at the hospital, Jorgee was talking to the *Kalinago* girl when Pauline walked in with Mr. Jenson. Jorgee's stomach flipped. He couldn't place whether it was the man's imposing height, deep voice or piercing grey eyes that unsettled him. He made small talk with the nurses and stopped by several beds before motioning for Jorgee to join them.

"I see you're feeling better, boy," Mr. Jenson remarked.

"Ye-ye-yes sir."

"Good." He asked a few more questions then brought up the fight. "Are you sure my boys attacked you?"

Jorgee looked at the floor, his heart hammering. "Yes, sir."

"They said you're lying."

Jorgee wasn't surprised. He shifted his gaze to the man's face. "It-it was them, sir. They always troubling me."

"You need to be careful with those accusations, boy. My sons are not troublemakers."

Jorgee felt a lump in his throat. "It was them."

"You also need to remember your mother works for me. I'm the one who feeds you. Understand?"

Embarrassed, Jorgee nodded.

Pauline interjected. "You need to tell the truth, Jorgee."

"Mammy, I not lying!"

"Lower your voice, boy," Mr. Jenson admonished.

There was an awkward silence. Jorgee looked at his mother, soundlessly pleading with her to side with him.

Mr. Jenson spoke. "I hope you get well soon and we find who attacked you." He lingered a while longer, then nodded at Pauline and walked away.

Both of them watched him leave. Pauline spoke to Jorgee. "You make me pass like a fool and it wasn't those boys that hit you."

"Why you believing them and you not believing me?"

"Because I never see them ill-treat you."

"They 'fraid their father. In school, they different."

"So nobody never report them, Jorgee? You hear the man talk about my job?"

Before Jorgee could reply, his twin friends, Brent and Slim, sauntered in with their mother to visit. Physically, they were as different as night and day, but they both backed up Jorgee's story.

Too quickly, Jorgee had to return to school. Pleading with his mother to change schools had gotten him nowhere. It was a clear day and children were playing in the yard when he arrived. Jorgee sat on a bench near his class and was pulling a comic book out of his new bag when someone slapped his head. Dread descended upon him. Two voices erupted in laughter and he smiled with relief.

"Come let's play football," urged Brent, the bigger of the twins.

Jorgee, still feeling dispirited, declined, but they convinced him soon enough. He put the book into his bag and joined them. They were still caught up in the game when the bell rang. Sweating, Jorgee dashed towards his classroom for his bag. It wasn't on the bench. It wasn't in the classroom. He felt anxious as he slowly took his place in the assembly area. Hearing a commotion, Jorgee turned and saw Kalid standing exactly behind him. Jorgee groaned inwardly. Being slightly taller, he felt Kalid's breath on his neck as he chanted:

*"Jorgee Porgie, cry-cry and poor*
*I'll tell my father you careless for sure.*
*You lose the bag he buy for you*
*And see the state of the brand-new shoe."*

Children snickered and tried to get a glimpse of Jorgee's dusty shoes.

"Those shoes were too ugly for me so I gave them to Jorgee's mother, our housekeeper." Laughing, he pushed the back of Jorgee's knees, and Jorgee lurched forward causing a stir.

Jorgee's eyes welled, but recalling his mother's words, he spun and lunged at Kalid. They rolled on the courtyard, long limbs entwined. Grabbing. Punching. Scratching. Grunting. Jorgee soon found himself warding off Krisan too. Students circled them in a frenzy, some screaming fearfully, some in excitement.

Teachers separated them and brought them to the principal's office. Jorgee's skin burned with scratches; his heart hammered; his shirt was missing buttons;

his collar was halfway torn; but he felt proud. The Jenson boys, equally dishevelled, regarded him with contempt. Mr. David, the principal, forced a feeble apology out of them then addressed the previous attack on Jorgee. Kalid vehemently denied involvement, while Krisan sniffled with his head bowed, blowing on his knuckles to ease the sting of bruises.

Just then the janitor knocked the door. He held up a bag, soiled and sooty. "That's mine!" Jorgee exclaimed.

The janitor raised his chin at the Jenson brothers. "I see these two throw it earlier, and I thought it was garbage."

"It wasn't us!" Kalid's nose flared, and his chest rose and fell. His narrowed eyes darted aimlessly. Krisan continued blowing his knuckles. The janitor was insistent and finally Kalid admitted the truth.

They were sent back to class, but when Jorgee saw his mother and Mr. Jenson walking across the courtyard the next day, his heart started racing. The boys were called back to the office. Jorgee could feel the Jensons' grey eyes on him. He sat on the plastic chair next to his mother. The Jensons remained standing. Mr. David sat behind his desk and gave a synopsis of what happened, but Mr. Jenson said his sons were falsely accused.

Jorgee was sure everyone could hear his heartbeat. "A-a-accused?"

"My boys said Jorgee threw the new bag, which I bought him, into the incinerator and blamed it on them. He even tried to destroy the new shoes we gave him."

Jorgee heard his mother gasp. He hoped she didn't believe those lies. Breathing heavily, he cried, "I wouldn't destroy my shoes! And I didn't throw my bag!"

Mr. Jenson shook his head and addressed the principal. "This boy is a liar and that cannot be tolerated at this school. I demand an apology."

Pauline and the principal objected at the same time. Mr. David raised his palm. "To be fair, Mr. Jenson," he said. "I saw Jorgee playing football. The janitor saw your boys throw the bag, and they admitted to it. They are the ones who attacked Jorgee the other day, and they are the ones who should be punished."

Jorgee looked at the brothers. Their eyes were glued to the floor.

Mr. Jenson cleared his throat. "Boys?"

Silence.

"Boys!" Mr. Jenson's voice boomed across the office, his eyes blazing.

The floodgates opened. "Sorry." Their voices shook and their heads remained bowed.

Mr. Jenson pointed at them. "Let this be my final warning to both of you!" In a softer tone he addressed Jorgee. "My apologies."

Mr. David asked to speak with the Jensons privately, and Pauline and Jorgee exited the office into bright sunshine. She said, "I working on something, Jorgee. Things will get better."

When Jorgee got home that evening, he was about to shift the curtain to enter their bedroom, but stopped when he heard voices. Standing in the small living area, he listened intently.

"Today is the last day you'll treat us like dirt, Jenson," said his mother. We deserve better."

Mr. Jenson hardly came to their house. He muttered something.

"I'm done with the secrecy, done with working for you." Pauline's voice sounded triumphant. Intrigued, Jorgee leaned close to the partition that separated their bedroom and living room.

"You'll be sorry," said Mr. Jenson.

"Humph! Your father got me a new job, and now he's my lawyer. So it's you who will be sorry, Jenson."

Jorgee's curiosity was piqued even more.

"M-m-my father?" stammered Jenson.

"Yes, the man you don't like," said Pauline. "The one you see when you look at Jorgee."

"But why do you need a lawyer?"

"To take you to court for child support."

Jenson scoffed. "W-w-where is all this coming from?"

"I'm sick and tired of your treatment, Jenson! You want to keep this a secret, but unless you pay up, I'm going to tell your wife."

Jorgee jumped as a hand struck the partition, causing it to vibrate.

"No! No, Pauline, you cannot do that! You want to destroy me after all I'm doing for you?"

"Doing what? Making empty promises? The way you treat Jorgee hurts me. He deserves better! See what happening with the boys. They need to know the truth!"

Jorgee's heart hammered. What truth?

"In time, Pauline. In time."

"Eleven years is enough time. You need to admit that Jorgee is your son and accept responsibility as his father. Either that or we going to court."

Jorgee sank to the floor, his eyes wide and misty, and his heart exploding. This man, his father? Those boys, his brothers?

"Noooooo!" he howled, pounding the partition.

He heard rushed footsteps and brushed his mother off when she tried to embrace him. Teary eyed, Jenson looked on.

# Aussies In The Stadium

The battle was between the "Windies" and the "Aussies." It was the first time that the boys from down under were playing in Dominica. The great Australian cricket team was indeed here and had been strutting their stuff for the past three days. Today was day four and the Windies were bowling. I was excited.

Early in the morning, the rain had made a brief appearance. But I was inwardly convinced that the weather would improve later, when I would be going to the stadium to experience the 4th day of Test Cricket, 26th April, 2012.

It was the second time that I was going to be a spectator at an international cricket game. The first time, it had been a high school outing. My form was taken to the Windsor Park to see the Windies and… it was so long ago; I no longer remember who they were playing against. But I know that I had a wonderful time. We had travelled from Portsmouth, a group of happy Fourth formers, and I was elated to have been part of that special group. We had entered the park all hyped up and ready to enjoy every scintillating moment. I had no idea of the game rules but that had not been a hindrance. Just being in the park with all those diehard fans, I was sure that I would comprehend somehow. I was determined to go with the flow—jump, shout, or wail, as was necessary. I was lucky, because my Spanish teacher had chosen to stand next to me and so, for that day, I was tutored by a genuine connoisseur of the game. I was a fast learner, and the information explained was clear. Cricket was theory coupled with practical

JERMAINIA COLAIRE-DIDIER lives in Dominica and has been a French lecturer for over 25 years. She holds a Masters' Degree in Translation and Terminology and is passionate about the French language, as well as creative writing. Her dream is to publish her work in English and in French.

application. I learnt the terms, maiden, over, leg-before-wicket and all the vocabulary that went along with cricket commentary.

This time around, I was hoping to wade through because I was alone. Nonetheless, I was bent on enjoying myself to the fullest. With prepaid ticket in hand I walked along Bath Road and headed for the stadium. I was dressed in white pants and an island shirt, wearing a wide brimmed hat for protection from the sun and carrying my Kalinago basket with some snacks and water. I was ready for a day of fun, no matter what.

Just as I was crossing into the first courtyard of the stadium, I heard a shout, "Ma Thomas!" I turned around and saw my friend Anisia from Soufriere. "I didn't know you going to cricket. I would have gone with you," she said. Anisia was even more prepared than me. An avid fan, she had her icebox and her packed lunch for the day.

"What ticket you have?" she quizzed.

"Oh, my ticket says John and Laurent stand," I answered.

"Eh ben, you and I cannot meet," Anisia said sadly. "I couldn't afford to pay thirty dollars every day, so I buy de cheaper ticket. But I still see. De only fing doh, is that at midday de sun does be in my eyes. But I love my cricket, so I doh mind. I just have to try to get a high seat."

"Ok," I said. "Enjoy the game. See you later." We both went our separate ways. She headed for the East Stand while I got ready to pass through security. Security was tight. Everyone was searched as they made their way through the entrance. The tragedy of 9/11 had surely changed the way things were done. But I had no problem with that.

Security scrutiny over, I headed for my stand. I climbed the steps and settled down at number 301, row 14, seat number one. Soon after a young man came along and took seat number two. There I sat, looking at the pitch. The air was pregnant with excitement. Souls hungry for a win were quickly filling up the stadium. All wanted the Windies, our boys, to perform, and they had come to support in full force. In fact, our own son of the soil, Shane Shillingford, was playing! Imagine the pride of a whole nation! We were so believing that something great would happen. I could feel the ripples of anticipation all around me.

The stadium was alive. A crescendo of animated voices could be heard. Some fans were predicting a victory for the West Indies, while others were a bit more guarded in their opinions. Some of the animation could readily be associated with the alcohol which patrons were happily ingesting. The Kubuli, the Red Cap, the Presidente, all formed part of the happy drinking mélange. Then, there was the scent of food—barbeque chicken, sizzling sausages on sticks, bakes frying, peleau. The menu was quite varied. Some patrons were coming in with their bags of fresh popcorn in hand and their bottles of cold soda. Cricket in the Caribbean was really a festival!

Then there was the overwhelming presence of the number one sponsor DIGICEL. Red and white paraphernalia was abundant. There were red plastic clappers making enough noise by themselves, head ties, red number cards with a big SIX or FOUR written in white, and of course, the talk of the crowd. The Digi girls with their skinny white tights and red T-shirts were showing off their bodies and decorated faces. The Digicel crew could be seen moving from one place to another, led by a man dressed in a green outfit and blowing a horn. Another man was waving a large flag of Dominica as the group went from stand to stand. Smaller Dominican flags could be seen all over the place.

The stadium looked quite colourful with its yellow, red and orange seats. It was a thrilling experience to be in such an environment. For so long in Dominica, we had been restricted to just seeing the pictures of other people's stadiums on our television sets. But no longer! We were now proud owners of a great sporting space and visitors from around the globe were impressed with it. The World Creole Music Festival had seen to that.

Indeed, the Chinese had executed an excellent job. The speed, precision and professionalism exhibited by these Asian workers were attributes to be emulated by our work men here in Dominica. The beauty of the stadium was amazing. Added to this, was the view of the majestic green mountains rising on both sides of the Roseau Valley, which spectators could admire from their seats. Indeed, the Nature Isle was on show, and I felt a sense of pride being Dominican. As I looked to my left, I beheld the big, white cross, serene and comforting perched at Morne Bruce. And to my right, one could admire some of the houses in Goodwill.

At last the game began. In the beginning, the rhythm was slow. But one by one the runs began adding up. Suddenly there was a unanimous cry. "Bowled!" It was 10:22 a.m., and the first wicket for the Aussies had fallen.

The bowler was Shane Shillingford of Dublanc, a Dominican making a name for himself and his country. There was wild joy among his supporters for this breakthrough. Good job! He had so far taken seven wickets in the series.

The horns began to blow, the exuberant shouts and whistles could be heard all over. Delirious, I joined in the excitement.

The game continued. The sky was slightly overcast, and I prayed that it could stay that way. There were vendors dressed in their yellow tops, red caps and black pants, going around selling Jamaican patties, drinks, and water. Groups of school children decked out in uniforms came flocking in from time to time. Here and there an officer of the law could be seen. On the field, the Aussies were slowly but surely amassing their runs. Then it was again Shane's time to bowl. The stadium quivered with anxiety. We all counted on Shane to do it again; he seemed a fitting saviour. Then, "*Baam!!!*" Another wicket was taken. This time, however, it had been taken by Deonarine, the Trinidadian. Again, the crazy joy of happy Dominicans could be seen and felt. With eight wickets down there were two more to go. I hoped that they would soon fall.

Suddenly, I heard some commotion to my right. I looked over and to my surprise I heard someone shouting, "Laugh now, but we will good for all you just now." I could not believe my ears. You mean a Dominican (West Indian by extension) would see fit to come support the other team? And be so brave to come sit in a crowd of "All de way with Windies fans?" The man's outburst was greeted with disdain. Even I said to myself, "*Why doesn't the man go and sit down with the Australian group in the other stand? I would have liked to see how they would welcome his company.*"

Some people were voicing their displeasure with the man. He then stood up and continued ranting "I can sit down where I want, I pay my money for my ticket. Australia going to beat those jokers so bad." At the same time, it was quite amusing to see a lady next to him waving a big flag and shouting, "Go Windies, go!" I joined in the refrain. I wanted to keep hope alive against all odds.

But the Aussies were coming on strong, and the pressure was on. Australia was stretching it out as much as they could. They wanted to make sure that our boys would be left with a big lead to follow. All part of the game, I guess.

Just as my mind was beginning to wander, there was an exhilarating explosion of excitement all around me. Shane had taken another wicket! What joy! I jumped, shouted, danced, and let myself participate fully in that wonderful moment. Imagine, conservative me! No one could have thought that my knowledge of the game was minimal. Maybe I could not explain in detail the intricate rules of the game, but I knew when someone was bowled. And even if I did not know, the pandemonium which had broken out in the stands left me no choice. Something wonderful was happening. The Windies were now hyped up and giving the Australians a run for their money. Three hundred and fifty-one runs for eight!

Some people in the middle stand were doing the Mexican wave. As row after row rose and then sat down in unison, a sense of satisfaction and pride welled up within me. I remembered, the bible quote: "How good and pleasant it is for brethren to dwell together in unity." Yes, it was indeed beautiful to see, so many of my fellow countrymen enjoying themselves in such a wholesome fashion. If only that attitude could be transferred to the other areas of our civil lives.

The atmosphere was charged while we waited for the last wicket to fall. The dissenting voices of the few unhappy "Aussie/Dominican" fans could not stifle the exuberance of joy which was being expressed by the majority. The whistles, the horn, the "Go Windies chant," the plastic clappers—it was the happy noise of an expectant crowd.

Then it happened. "Bowl him!" The last wicket was no more. It was 11:22 a.m. Shane had taken his tenth wicket. What a feat! What a treat for all Dominicans. What a morning! Shane had given us a show, something to remember forever. A big placard with the words "Shane Takes Ten" was being paraded through my stand by a happy fan. The woman next to me could not contain herself. Her short stubby body could be seen swaying from side to side as she waved her Dominican flag.

Yes, the Aussies had come, they had played. But on day four, history had been made…by Shane.

# Truth Or Scare

I wiped angrily at the fresh tears pouring from my eyes. After another long, hot Saturday at the Roseau market, the scent of various garden produce—chiefly chive, guava and mangoes, mixed with the stench of perspiration—was overwhelming.

A few of the other passengers on the bus tried to strike up a conversation with me.

"You that's the granddaughter for Marie, nuh? Josephine child, Deidra?" But I was not in the mood. My curt replies cut all efforts at chit-chat short.

Dense forests, precipices, road-side shops and animals grazing contentedly, passed by in a blur as I stared out the bus window. I was so mad at my parents. This was not the way my two-week Easter break was supposed to go! I was planning to have an awesome break with my friends, but my parents thought it would be better if I went to the countryside to spend some time with our relatives there. "*Especially as Granny was sick*," they said. So here I was, on my way to Delices, also known to me as "Behind God's Back."

"Look, you reach," said the bus driver. "Not by Ma Marie you say you going, nuh?"

He was wearing a beaten *chapeau paille* and a green, wrinkled t-shirt which bore the words "I Am Dominica." He tapped his fingers on the steering wheel impatiently. I scrambled to gather my belongings and paid him. Then I got off the bus, lugging my heavy bags. I could feel all eyes on my back, and heard whispered speculations as to why I was crying, and why it had been so long since I last visited.

MICHELLE ALLYSHIA BELLE, a Dominican who currently resides in China, has been exposed to a kaleidoscope of people, cultures, and life experiences. As a young black woman, her writing is seasoned with the rhythmic vibrancy of her African-Caribbean roots while capturing a kaleidoscope of universal thoughts, fantasies, hopes and fears.

I ignored them and sucked my teeth loudly as I turned to walk up the dirt path with hibiscus and ginger lilies planted on either side leading to my grandmother's house. A final glance back at the departing bus revealed an elderly man in the back seat grinning at me, his smile sporting as many gaps as there were potholes in the road.

The flat, yellow and white house was filled with laughter and chattering, but a second of silence ensued as I walked through the door. Then everyone started talking at once.

"Look. Deidra reach!" my cousin Kevin exclaimed.

"Welcome DeeDee!" Aunty Rose chimed in.

"How was the ride?" asked another.

And then, "Eh, eh. DeeDee, *doudou mwen*! Come and give Granny a kiss." I crossed the room and awkwardly obliged, putting down my bags by the door.

"Kevin, go and bring her bags in the room," Aunty Rose said to her son.

While thinking about what I would have been doing if I was back home in Goodwill, I picked up snatches of gossip from the conversation: a YouTube video about the character who had stolen Ma Dadda's two female goats, Curtis and his affair with his wife's cousin, and Ma Erika's—one of the village's most notorious *soukouyans*—latest shenanigans. The adults seemed oblivious to my discomfort as they fired questions at me, and my cousins were in their own world, playing and joking with each other. So I just slumped further into the old, lumpy chair and tried to pretend I was somewhere else. No doubt about it, these were going to be the longest two weeks of my life.

Nightfall brought with it the tranquillity of country life. I remembered how much I used to like being in Delices before. My days were filled with jumping rope, trips to White River, playing marble-hole and climbing all sorts of trees. The aroma of the cornmeal in our bowls tickled my nose as I savoured the taste of *bwaden* (bay leaf), nutmeg and coconut milk in every spoonful. The faint sound of music from the bar down the road wafted on the breeze. Crickets chirped incessantly, and the moon struggled to be seen through a cloudy sky. It was a particularly windy evening and the trees in the yard swayed and bowed. My cousins and I were all gathered around Granny, who sat comfortably in her special chair, which no one else was allowed to sit on. Some of us were cramped on benches on the small porch, and some were sitting on the front steps, but we were all within earshot. There was a brief silence as we dug in to our porridge.

"Granny tell us a witch story!" squeaked Tyron from the corner.

"Yes!" voices shouted in unison.

"Hello! Too loud!" Aunty Rose scolded from inside. Her eyes were glued to 'Scandal' on the television. "And just now is bed time, eh."

Sucking of teeth and grumbling followed the announcement of the impending bed time.

"But I tell allu so much already," Granny said. "Mind allu cannot sleep after that," she warned jokingly.

She lay her head back on the chair. She looked more tired than usual and sounded slightly out of breath. Her red and yellow flowered dress was tucked between her legs, and her once rosy cheeks were sagging and wrinkled. Gray hair in neat plaits sat atop her head, but her eyes were still the liveliest feature of her face, light brown and all-seeing.

"I'm not afraid. Besides, I doh believe in those things," I boasted.

Granny really did not look very well. A worry line creased her forehead.

"*Zanfan mwen*, they real. Let me tell you why…"

We all scrambled forward, eager to hear. Maybe the others were shivering on the inside, but not me. I thought it was fun to listen, even if what she said about soukouyans was all nonsense. "Folklore" was what my Literature teacher called it.

"A late afternoon I go by the river for some water," Granny began. "Darkness end up meeting me there. On the way back home, I hurrying, boy, 'cause is me alone. And guess what I see?"

"A soukouyan!" Alliane screamed.

"No, a lougawou!" Keyan countered.

"La Diablesse," Granny whispered. "I see a pretty woman sitting on a big stone. I don't know what she was looking for, but she put her head down, like she looking for something on the ground. As I reach by her, I look down too. And what I see? One horse foot was under her dress. Bondyé! I forget buckets of water and I run! Is a good thing I had on my panty wrong side out, and I left-handed. And as I running, I praying loud!"

"So she didn't run behind you?" I asked, gripping Granny's hand.

"I thought you didn't believe in those things," my cousin Keyan mocked.

"I don't. I-I'm just asking what happened in the story," I mumbled.

Granny laughed then coughed, a dry, racking sound. "No, my child. I was lucky. I doh know. All I know is I get home safe, shaking like a leaf. When I tell Mama what I see, she forget about the bucket and give me some Psalms to pray. She say is God that watch over me. So you see, DeeDee, I see, I believe."

After bombarding Granny with all kinds of questions, we sat, breathing heavy, hearts racing and eyes wide. We had subconsciously huddled closer, and I know every one of us was scared. Outside seemed to get even darker, as a cloud covered the moon's weak light completely for a few seconds. Granny looked exhausted from the storytelling, and she laid her head back against the chair again. Alliane and I were having our own little tête-à-tête when I noticed Kevin glancing at me. When he caught my eye, he feigned innocence, and turned back to their little circle, lowering his voice.

Curious, I strained my ears, trying to catch snippets of their conversation. Kimon smiled at me and said, "Deidra, come and hear that. You say you not afraid of them ting, right? Hmph! Let's bet you 'fraid to go by the river now to see."

"Ouch!" I hissed under my breath as my big toe bounced on one of the wooden wardrobe legs. It took all my will-power to not curse out loud. When I looked out the window, it was dark, except for the pale moonlight slithering through the thick clouds. A faint snore from Granny caused me to pause in my tracks. After making sure she was asleep, I continued to tip-toe outside. Crouching low behind the sweet lime bush at the front of the house, black hoodie pulled over my head, a million thoughts ran through my mind. Why did I agree to my cousins' stupid dare? Because I wanted to prove that I wasn't scared, that's why. So now I had to go to that same river that Granny told us about in her story, where she met the *La Diablesse*, and return with some proof that I had indeed reached there. My cousins were supposed to meet me by the sweet lime tree at midnight. They would wait for me by the ravine while I went on my mission, but no one had showed up yet. Maybe they had not heard the living room clock chime. I was thinking that if they did not show up soon, I could go back indoors, when I jumped at the sound of approaching footsteps. There they stood, grinning like the three stooges, Kevin, Kimon and Alliane. My heart plummeted as we all ambled up the road.

When I glanced back, I realised that my cousins were now almost invisible, engulfed by the heavy darkness. I pep-talked myself as I walked, chin up, shoulders squared. Just in case of trouble, I was equipped with cloves of garlic, a silver rosary, a small bottle of Holy Water, and a flashlight. I got to the river without incident. To be on the safe side, I kept reciting the twenty-third Psalm, 'The Lord Is My Shepherd,' aloud as I picked up a few handfuls of wet stones and sand from the river bank, stuffed them into the plastic bag I brought along, and ran back in the direction I came from. Two more bends in the road and I would be back by the ravine.

I thought I had imagined it when I saw a red streak of light fly past my line of vision. "No, not a ball of fire!" I thought, quickening my pace. Then it flew by again! I turned around at the sound of footsteps behind me. The rushing of the river could still be heard, but faintly now. I began to jog, looking behind me every few steps, but I stopped short at the sight ahead of me. My heart beat was deafening as it pounded in my ears. I felt wobbly, as my knees suddenly got weak and rubbery. My mouth opened to scream, but my throat locked. Only a hoarse whisper came out. It looked like the outline of a woman, but her features were not really defined; just a black outline, in a long, flowing dress, with blood-red eyes. Eyes which stared straight at me as she—it—seemed to float just off the ground.

My mind was blank as I stood, rooted to the spot, entranced by those red eyes, feeling light-headed. An owl hooted somewhere in the distance, and in a split second I untied the plastic with the sand and reached into my pocket for the Holy Water. Taking a deep breath, I lunged towards her, flung the sand and stones at the eyes and doused her with Holy Water.

A howl came out then, a throaty, animal-like growl that simultaneously sounded like a woman's high-pitched scream. I did not stop nor turn around again. The clouds shifted suddenly and the entire stretch before me lit up. Out of the corner of my eye, I noticed a scrap of red and yellow cloth partly wedged under a rock, looking very out of place, but still vaguely familiar. Adrenaline pumped through my veins, fuelling my weakened body as I ran. I ran until, gasping and flustered, I collapsed at my cousins' feet, by the wall next to the ravine.

My cousins began to fire questions at me. Finally, composed, I relayed my story to them in fine detail. All eyes were on me and mouths agape, then, all of a sudden, they all started laughing. They thought I was joking!

Kimon howled with laughter. "So Deidra, because you were too COWARD to make it to the river you make up that nonsense story?"

"You not easy, nuh, girl," Alliane giggled.

"I serious! Why would I lie?" I protested. "I did reach the river, and I got wet stones and sand. But I saw a REAL soukouyan on the way back and I threw them at her. For true! If I lie, I curse God!"

I could not believe they thought I was lying.

"Deidra is a scaredy cat," Kimon taunted.

"I'm not!" I insisted. But I was too upset from my encounter by the river to say more as we trudged back home on the darkened road.

The morning sun assaulted my half-closed eyes as I turned over on the couch. Last night I was so tired that I fell asleep in the living room right on the sofa. I had been awakened from sleep by the sound of running footsteps and harried talking. Squinting against the sunlight, I sat up as I watched my aunties packing what looked like bed linen into a large bag. Uncle Bill darted into Granny's bedroom carrying a wet cloth and a mug of what smelled like coffee. My cousins appeared around the same time, rubbing their eyes and yawning.

"What happen?" I asked in concern.

A siren's wail in the distance seemed to be coming closer.

"Granny," Aunty Marian uttered before dashing into the bedroom again.

"What's wrong with Granny?"

"She sick. Nurse Joyce called the ambulance, they on their way."

As if on cue, the ambulance parked in front of the yard, and four well-built men scurried inside carrying a stretcher. By now, neighbours had gathered around, some still in bed clothes, whispering among themselves. Uncle Bill and Aunty Rose climbed into the ambulance after the stretcher on which Granny lay moaning, skin red and blotchy and eyes closed, was carefully placed. Aunty Marian stood with us, watching it retreat, tears rolling down her face.

"Élas, Mama in plenty pain. Plenty pain," she cried out.

My cousins and I, sad and bewildered, exchanged knowing looks. The siren's blare became softer and softer, until the sound disappeared altogether. That was the last time I saw my grandmother alive, and the memory of that

Easter break would be etched into the crannies of my mind forever. The nagging truth had settled in the pit of my stomach like a ton of cement. I tried to deny it, but it gnawed at me, leaving me queasy. I guess there's truth to "Folklore" after all. But sometimes, what you don't want to see in front of your door, you may actually end up finding under your bed!

# One of Him Own

Not one soul could sleep a wink de night we did put Sergeant Vincent Murphy in de ground. We couldn't sleep, but we couldn't walk round much neither. Since Hurricane Maria hit our little island three months ago, rain fall harder than hammer on nail head, as if it intend to drown de rest of we altogether. So me and de fellas gather down by Ma Daryl's bar near de Deep Water Harbour to warm de night with some cheap rum.

Wilson had ask Vincent's younger brother, Lenny, to join we after de funeral wake, and de poor boy did scared to say no. He say they have some business to discuss, and Lenny just nod his head and come along. Wilson tend to have that effect on people, his shoulders big and broad from hauling nets of fish into his speedboat from sun up to sun down. He was a man of few words, except when he had one too many drinks. Then his voice was a deep baritone, like Barry White, so he only need to say something once and you bound to obey. But beyond that, he was a loyal friend, especially to Vincent. Them two did closer than two peas in a pod from they did young.

Ma Murphy, Vincent's mother, used to say, "Them six in one, half a dozen in de other."

They had make First Communion together at St. Alphonsus Catholic Church when they did only boys, and Wilson was Vincent's best man at his wedding six years ago. Ma Murphy had to ring Vincent's ears during de ceremony to get him to pay attention. Him and Wilson did laugh so hard, he didn't even realise de whole

YAKIMA CUFFY hails from Dominica, the Nature Island of the Caribbean. She is an award-winning writer, poet and play-wright. A lawyer by profession, the prominent themes in her writing include patriotism, West Indian identity, migration, faith and sensuality. Some of her work may be found on her Facebook handle, *Yakima July*.

church was waiting on him to say "I do." What was so funny, only de two of them did know. Is a good ting Noreen wasn't a fussy girl, or else she would have storm out de church hall right then and there with his ring still in her pocket.

Yes, them did so close in life we all thought Vincent's death would break Wilson. De night we got de news, Wilson didn't say a word. But then again, it was not so unusual for him to say nothing. He sat on a bar stool at Ma Daryl's with his hands on his knees staring out de window at de silver sea, how it clamber onto the shore like a deluge of broken dreams, then retract lazily again. And then, suddenly, he cup his face with his hands and wept. It was a sight I can't forget, to see a man de size of a mountain unravel before me very eyes. I did feel for him. We all did lose a friend that night, but Wilson, he did lose a brother.

Lenny did lose a brother too, although you couldn't really tell. I suppose he did so used to missing Vincent it come like a part of him now, so he don't need to cry and carry on. He did look more out of place than mournful, with his grey cashmere sweater button up to his neck and black rubber boots on his foot, as though rain was some disease to be protected from. It was easy to tell he come from foreign. He did look shiny in a place of dull tings, like de porcelain tea set me Granny did keep in she cabinet away from de likes of we children. Except for his svelte stature, Lenny did look nothing like Vincent either. In de haze of de kerosene lamp, he did look as yellow as de tasty curry Ma Daryl make on Friday afternoons. Rumour have it their mother had an affair with a Syrian merchant back in de early 80s and Lenny come nine months later. But his father never claim him, so nobody ever know whether that story was true or not.

That was another usual ting round here, children not knowing who their fathers were. And that never stop Ma Murphy from believing her sons was destined for greatness—that they was somehow "better" than de rest of we. She always boast how Lenny doing so well in London, but this de first time he come home since he left Dominica bout fifteen years ago, and she could never tell you what he doing over there that got him so busy.

Yes, Ma Murphy did proud to a fault. When Vincent join de Police Force ten years ago, she say she son going to become de next Commissioner of Police. He move out de slums of Tarish Pit soon after and marry his high school sweetheart, Noreen. From that time onward, he did try to prove that he was no longer one of we, but we never pay him no mind. With a mother like Ma Murphy, a man bound to live his life behind a mask. Is that kind of thinking that have Vincent where he is right now, bless his soul.

Tonight, Ma Daryl's was full of grievers. Some of de men them was drowning their sorrows with beer while some was playing dominoes beneath de kerosene lamp in one corner of de bar. And de rain lash heavy, heavy against de tarpaulin that now serve as a ceiling, forming pockets of water between de rafters. Before, we used to jump and squirm when de rain hit de tarpaulin so hard. De hurricane did make us paranoid. But we get used to de sound now since rain fall day and night round here.

"I heard that there has been a lot of funerals in the last couple of weeks," Lenny blurt over Hurricane's calypso "Wounded Lion" that was blasting from de little transistor radio perch on a stall above we heads. "Noreen told me insurance companies are caving, and people have been laid off from their jobs. Everyone is tense and worried about how they're going to get their roofs fixed. Seems the hurricane continues to claim victims long after it has passed, innit?"

His proper British accent float on de cold sea breeze like de gloom of death—like an imposter we could only tolerate for a short while. He look at us confidently, as though he had just unearth some grand revelation.

"It ain't only de stress that killing people round here, boy," I say while slamming down a domino on de little wooden table we did crouch round.

"J.J., you better hush up!" Tehani, one of de younger men order. "De boy don't need to know bout all of that."

"Know about what?" Lenny ask, his curiosity now at it pique.

"Boy, what you ain't know can't hurt you," Charles, who we call Charlo, say in jest. Charlo always cracking a joke. He did call himself a farmer, selling a crocus bag of provisions bout de place, but to this date I ain't know one piece of land that he own. Tehani say Charlo de only farmer he know that can't tell de difference between a plantain and a banana tree.

"I'm not a boy! I'm a grown man, and I want to know what you all are talking about."

I look across at Wilson. He was sitting on a bar stool close to us holding a shot glass in his right hand and swirling de amber drink in it round in a circular motion. Even in de dim light, I could tell it was cask rum—one of them local ones old men make by distilling fresh sugar cane and then leaving it to age together with spice, bay leaves and snake oil in mahogany barrels. I learn not to mess round with cask rum a long time ago; it sweet and mellow to de mouth but leave you feeling like you did get hit by a truck de next day. I know any man who drink cask rum in one gulp de way Wilson do ain't fit to fight nobody, so I decide to take me chance.

I look back at Lenny and ask, "How Noreen tell you you brother die?"

Without hesitation, he respond, "She said he died of a stroke."

"A stroke eh?" mock Charlo. "He did have high blood pressure?"

We all laugh, leaving poor Lenny in a state of confusion.

"Why allya have de young man so discombobulated? If you going to set him wise, just tell him already," Tehani scold we.

Tehani was a joiner by profession, but he could easily have been a lawyer if his family had de money. He like to read big books and use words like discombobulated and ostentatious.

"Well, Lenny, your big shot brother was on patrol duty after de hurricane. De Prime Minister had declare a State of Emergency on de island and had we lock up in our homes from 4:00 p.m. till 6:00 a.m. It was like everybody did going mad. People looting stores and supermarkets, stealing vehicles and furniture from warehouses. It was like Armageddon, boy. And so, de Government did invite squads of police from all round de region to help maintain law and order. I hear they did give them authority to shoot on sight."

Wilson slam his glass down on de bar counter, and everyone look over their shoulder to see whether he was enrage.

"I'll have another," he instructed Ma Daryl, and she did as he command her.

So I continue with me story. "Lenny, you remember Laurel who live in de junction by Mr. Geoffery shop in Tarish Pit?"

"Of course I remember Laurel," he reply. "She used to sell ice pops at Goodwill School in the afternoons."

"Yes, same one. Well, about two weeks after de hurricane, Laurel youngest son, Akeem, and a group of other boys did went down Roseau during curfew to loot. Akeem did young in age but big in mind and body. They say he had a wheelbarrow of furniture dragging behind him when Vincent's police squad catch him. Rumour have it, Vincent did fire one warning shot in de air, and de boy did so arrogant and bad-mind he start pelt stone and empty beer bottle after de police. They say your brother give him one hot bullet in his leg, and all his friends them scatter and leave him bleeding on de ground."

"Serves him right! That boy must have been mad. He ought to have known that resisting arrest is a criminal offence," Lenny said.

"And Vincent ought to have know better than to kill one of him own!" Tehani yelled, standing to his feet and slamming his fist into de table so that his knuckles was a distension of pink flesh. "De boy did barely out his teens; barely got his mother breast milk off him face when your brother cut him down. It ain't right!"

"If y'all don't calm de hell down, you better go and find somewhere else to keep your buffoonery!" Ma Daryl exclaim in her high pitch voice.

Lenny's eyes did grow big like young calf that look upon its mother for de first time. "Killed him?" he mutter in disbelief.

I rest me hand on de boy's shoulder. "Yes. Vincent kill him."

Lenny shake he head.

It was hard for anyone to believe that Vincent could hurt a fly. Vincent was always de soft one, de smart one, de quiet one. In fact, it was Wilson that often protect him from being bullied at school or being roughed up by some of de gang members near their home. Ten years ago, when Vincent tell we that he was selected to join de Police Force, we was all in shock. None of we never thought that Vincent had de grit to be a police officer, but contrary to popular belief, Vincent soon move up de ranks to become a sergeant. Later, when Vincent tell we that he going to move out of Tarish Pit to a nicer community with his then fiancé, we was more relieved than proud. We did always fear that Tarish Pit would grind Vincent into something he was not— something more like de rest of we.

"It must have been a mistake," Lenny sob. He didn't even shed a tear at his brother funeral, but now, as Vincent's reputation lay in ruins before him, Lenny lament like a teenage girl after her first heartbreak.

"It's no mistake. If I never see it wid me own two eyes, I wouldn't have believe it neither," Tehani whisper. "De Government did give me an assignment to do repairs to some of their buildings, so I did have a curfew pass after de hurricane. I did just a few feet away when it happen. I watch as Vincent move closer to Akeem. I know your brother longer than I know me own self. I know he was trying to help de boy after he shoot him in de leg. He did call de ambulance straight away. But as he kneel on de ground beside

Akeem's quivering body, I see de boy spit in Vincent face. He tell your brother that he know who he truly is—that he just another bastard from Tarish Pit. He tell him he not better than any of we—that he just a big macko in a police uniform. Then Vincent stand up and stagger backwards, as if he was drunk with rage.

De other police officers was laughing hysterically. They start to say how Vincent must be fraid to put de boy in his place. But before them could say another word, we hear Vincent gun explode, and Akeem brains did all over de asphalt. His blood, red, and thick as me Granny's cornmeal porridge. I witness it meself."

We gasp as Tehani share his recollection. For a moment, de only ting we could hear was de sound of rain pounding against de tarpaulin overhead. De water pockets had get too heavy, so Ma Daryl take a long broomstick and poke at it to let de water run off outside. In one area, de water was so heavy it buss a hole through de tarpaulin and start spilling inside. Charlo help de old woman put a mop pail under de hole to collect de water.

"So, are you saying that because of what happened to Akeem, someone murdered my brother? Who was it? One of Akeem's gang members? Or was it Laurel herself?" Lenny ask, his voice trembling and his face a swollen, puffy mess.

"Boy, there are tings in this world stronger than any man. The kind of tings that does make healthy man just drop down dead for no reason. Forces. Evil forces. *Sorcière*," I say quietly.

And with that, Tehani start to explain, "J.J. right. I suspect is Laurel do it. I did go Akeem funeral. He was kin to me—our mothers did two brothers' children. You know Laurel is a dutty *soo-ti-weh*—she always encourage her children in their folly. Well, after de funeral, I did overhear de Priest warning she not to go to any *guardez-zafeh* to do no obeah on her son's killer. Father Cuthbert did tell she, "De Bible say, 'vengeance is mine, saith the Lord.'" But Laurel did look like she heart did done harden. I telling allya, I bet is she who do it."

Lenny start to laugh like he did losing his mind. "J.J., you expect an educated man like me to believe in witchcraft? That's preposterous!"

"Believe what you want boy, but we know for a fact that is not stress that kill Vincent, and it wasn't no bloody stroke neither!" Wilson bellowed.

"Are any of you doctors? How can you be so sure?"

Wilson chime again, "I know because Vincent's heart did strong as an ox. I know because we used to make love three times a week while Noreen was on nursing duty, and if what I gave him in bed didn't raise his pressure, there ain't a ting that could!"

The room hush immediately in sheer anticipation of what would happen next. I not sure whether it was de cask rum talking or whether Wilson just wanted to get it off his chest, but either way their secret was reveal to all of we that night, and Vincent not here to defend himself because he done dead and bury. We stare helplessly as an astonished Lenny struggle to align his brother's memory with these recent allegations. Suddenly, de pieces of de puzzle that was Sergeant Vincent Murphy was all starting to come together.

De men them start to laugh till them cry, but me only fix me eyes on Wilson, how de muscles in his face quiver with pain and his eyes did sore and red as Christmas sorrel. Wilson did love Vincent, and Vincent did love Wilson. But there was someting else de rest of de fellas didn't know. Someting I, Jeremy Joseph, would take to me grave, or else war would break loose in our beloved Tarish Pit.

De other boys that was with Akeem de night he die run home after them see de police put de bullet in his leg. They tell we some Jamaican police catch Akeem and shoot him in de leg, and that an ambulance coming to collect him to take him to de hospital. Me and all de fellas rush up to Princess Margaret to find out what happening. We say we come to give blood, but we well aware we don't qualify because we on de block every night smoking ganja. But when de ambulance reach, they tell us Akeem done dead, shot close range with a bullet to his head.

Straight away, I see Wilson leave casualty and step outside to make a phone call. He wait outside for bout ten minutes until a short, slim-face man dressed all in white come to meet him. I hear de man tell him to leave de money in a paper bag behind his house later that night, and when he put it down on de ground, never look back to see who take it. I hear de white-robed man warn him that obeah always come with a price. For some reason, I did get a funny feeling in me gut that de *guardez-zafeh* wasn't talking bout no dollars and cents.

And then, de unthinkable happen. I hear Wilson answer, "I willing to pay any price to avenge me son."

Me mouth did drop open when I hear him say so. As long as I live, I never see Wilson with the likes of any woman, much less to know he was Akeem's father. But like I did say before, most children round here never know their fathers anyway, or if they know they don't want to say.

Well, de morning after Akeem was killed, Tehani come give we de news that it was Vincent that shoot de boy dead. And when we hear this side of de story all of Tarish Pit was a bitter mob—all except Wilson. Wilson did wail and wail and wail until his eyes was empty, crusty wells. But de deed had already been done. He had unknowingly sign his lover's death warrant.

De torrents did coming down so strong tonight that de water in de mop pail did start to spill over and flood Ma Daryl's bar before we even recognise. By then, it did nearly ankle deep, so all of we had to get up and help to bail de water out. While me and Lenny was using pots and pans to throw de water out of Ma Daryl's plywood window, from de corner of me eye I notice Wilson staggering toward we. De water swished round his foot as he waded, but that wasn't the reason he did swaying from side to side. When he lean toward us, I did smell de hearty sweetness of cask rum on his breath. Brawny as he was, Wilson was never de kind of guy that could handle his liquor well.

He could barely look any of us in de eye, his countenance a brew of grief and guilt. Since Hurricane Maria, he did lose his roof, his son, and his lover too. I wonder how he bear it, to know that he punish Vincent for doing de very same ting he did—killing one of him own. I wonder if he tink revealing his secret would somehow absolve him. I wonder how different tings would have be if that blasted hurricane never come at all. These days, I wonder a lot of tings. But of one ting I am sure, I letting dead dogs lie, and I ain't saying a word of this to no one.

**Piton Noir Speculative Fiction Award** goes to Erwin Mitchel for *Tough Luck Jaco*. "Mitchel's entertaining story has set the gold standard for the next level of Dominican folktales. It is a nugget of anthropomorphic fantasy that takes the imagination along an adventure-filled walking trail, while never betraying how the journey ends."

# Tough Luck Jaco

On a mountain range overlooking the Melville Hall airport, lived a bird of spectacular plumage known as *Amazona arausiaca*. Pronunciation of his unique name proved difficult to most individuals, so he mostly went by an accepted nickname, "Jaco." A well-known big mouth, he loved to catch up on all the gossip amongst the animals and people. Through a unique adaptation, he was able to understand and speak human vernacular.

This self-proclaiming prince of his domain had a distinct blend of colours which made him stand out from other birds. He was also a very curious and assertive individual who commanded everyone's attention as he flew overhead. Jaco sometimes left his kingdom to visit his one true friend, King Sisserou, who he considered his only superior in beauty and grace. But Sisserou hated the spotlight, so his chosen habitat was secluded deep in the central forest reserve, an area known as Glo Gommier.

Every time a plane landed at the airport, Jaco would swoop down to be first in line to see the new arrivals. Then he would fly to the village and inform the locals on how the travellers looked or what they brought. Whenever an important person came to the island, he would tell Sisserou, but his friend was never interested due to his reclusive nature.

One day, while making his morning rounds on the airport, Jaco saw that the workers had assembled near the building and were in deep discussion.

"Boy, something big happening there, wii," he said to himself as he swooped in to eavesdrop.

ERWIN MITCHEL is an unpublished poet and short story writer from the remote village of Dipax, Castle Bruce. A fire fighter by profession, his favourite way to unwind is to grab a paper and pen. Next to his fiancée and two beautiful children, his greatest goal is to publish his lyrical creations.

They were talking about someone named Maria who was coming to the island, and they seemed very concerned. This caught Jaco's attention because he was usually first to broadcast any news, especially news of this extent. By the time he got to the village, all the locals were already talking about Maria and how she was set to arrive by 4 o'clock that same day. Jaco got very annoyed because his news had been "scooped" by others.

He retreated to the hills in order to brief the animals, but Mr. Toutwel and Sister Ramier had already begun to spread the word.

"But who tell dem about dat, nuh?" he said as he flew up to his nest.

Thus Jaco hatched a plan to be the first to see Maria in order to regain his superiority. At 3:30, Jaco went down to the airport. The eerie silence coupled with the absence of people pleased him because he thought he'd gotten there ahead of time. A strong wind swept across the airport as Jaco awaited Maria's landing.

"That is a big plane, wii," he said as he staggered to keep his perch. "I doh see it yet, but de headwind clearing de runway for landing," he grunted while being tossed about by the strengthening wind.

After two hours of waiting, Jaco realised that something was wrong. He decided to go home, but the wind did not permit flying. The prince found himself in a hazardous predicament. He was slammed, spun, poked, and battered by what he came to realise was a deadly storm. By a stroke of luck, he was thrown into a derelict fire truck at the end of the runway. Panic got the better of Jaco. His tiny heart hammered beyond control, and he collapsed inside the temporary refuge. This was a sad and confusing time for Prince Jaco. Unconscious and stranded, pandemonium reigned in his feathery head that night.

A forceful rumbling awakened Jaco the next morning. A low flying airplane had arrived to scout the area. As he stumbled out of the truck that had perhaps saved his life, he beheld a place that he no longer recognised. The airstrip itself was the only indication that he was still within his own kingdom. Attempting to gain altitude in order to remap, Jaco realised that most of his plumage had been taken away, so he could no longer fly. The once elegant and proud prince now resembled a worn bass broom. He had no idea which way to go because every tree, rock, river and road around him had been overturned.

The subjugated Prince rested in the faint morning sunlight in order to gather his strength and to formulate an action plan. He decided that the best place of refuge for him would be at King Sisserou's kingdom, but how to get there? Jaco had never travelled by foot before, and he perceived that his short legs were no good to this cause. Perhaps he could ask for directions as he went, or even trick someone into carrying him to Glo Gommier. So he started along his journey. Inch by inch he shuffled till he reached the village where he was astonished to see that it had suffered the same fate as his beloved kingdom! The locals spoke of Maria and blamed her for all the destruction. Whoever this Maria was, Prince Jaco was extremely upset by her behaviour.

The directions given to Jaco by the villagers took him to a crossroad intersection at an area called Pagua. It seemed an abandoned place. There was no one in sight to ask for help and the river had flooded most of the road. After a moment, a voice called out to him. "Jaco!" Startled, he turned to see who it was, but there was no one there. Just as he began to think that it was the wind, the voice called again "Jaco." It seemed to get closer, but who could it be?

It was apparent that Jaco's dilemma had caught the attention of Tèt Chien. He was a resident Boa constrictor snake whose main desire was to have a royal meal of plucked parrot. This stealthy serpent had been silently trailing Jaco from the beginning of his pilgrimage. Realising that the prince wasn't sure which way to go, he slithered out of the bushes to offer assistance.

"Where you going, boy?" he asked as he inched forward and tasted the air with his intrusive tongue.

"Well, I heading up Glo Gommier," said Jaco. "Maria mash up my home, so I going to stay by Sisserou for a while," he explained. Cautiously, he waddled to the side so Tèt Chien could pass by.

"You serious?" replied the snake as he contemplated the opportunity to eat both royal birds at once. Tèt Chien paused in silent thought.

"You know where he living, man?" asked Jaco, who was still a bit confused. "I never walk to go up there yet, nuh. Normally is fly I does fly."

"Yeah, man. Sisserou and myself is good fren," hissed the smiling serpent. "All now so is he I going and check before I go town by my brother."

Jaco seemed pleased that Tèt Chien was going the same route, but he found it odd that he claimed to be friends with Sisserou. "How comes mister saying the king is his fren, and I never meet him up there, nuh," whispered Jaco as he composed himself so as not to alarm Tèt Chien.

"So we moving together?" asked the serpent. He tasted the air and slithered ahead.

"Yeah, man, I coming," replied Jaco. He lurched alongside the suspicious serpent, being sure never to turn his back.

This unlikely pair of travellers caught the attention of everyone they passed along the way. Most found it odd that a snake and a parrot could be allies. The further they travelled the more obvious it became that the entire island had been vandalised by Maria. They came upon a river where a group of indigenous Kalinago people were gathered to bathe and cook. The Kalinago seemed quite happy to see Jaco—they all stood up and smiled at him. Tèt Chien, on the other hand, was wise enough to conceal himself.

"Where you going, parrot?" called the leader of the Kalinago. Jaco looked around and realised that he was standing alone.

The prince had never interacted with Kalinago people before, so he was uncertain what to expect. "Just up de road, man," he replied.

"You looking hungry. We have food there, wii. Come and sit down, nuh!" shouted the chief.

Jaco knew that he was handicapped by his short legs and that he was unable to fly away, so he accepted the invitation. Moments after perching himself on a rock, he noticed an area full of feathers similar to those of Sister Ramier. He also couldn't ignore that peculiar scent coming from the boiling pot, set between three stones. Then the Indians began to speak excitedly in their native language.

"What funny language dat, nuh?" muttered Jaco to himself. He couldn't comprehend what they were saying.

Discerning the impending danger, Jaco declared that his friend Tèt Chien was also hungry, and he was hiding nearby in a hollow tree. For some reason the Kalinagos seemed quite animated by this news.

"Where's him?" asked the leader as they dashed about in search of Tèt Chien.

This gave Jaco a window to slip away unnoticed. With his pounding heart racing ten paces ahead of him, he resumed his journey. He didn't get this far by being dumb; he knew that the snake really wanted to eat him. He continued on route for hours, slowly waddling around, over, and under countless obstacles. But nothing looked familiar. Jaco took this opportunity to practice a few things he planned to say, if ever he would meet Maria.

A familiar voice called out to him just as dusk began to settle across the battered landscape. "Jaco, garçon, I say you die, wii."

"Me? Die? What can kill me?" Jaco replied, looking around to see who it was.

It was friend Opossum, better known as Manicou, the guy who cleaned the trees and forest floor at Sisserou's kingdom.

Jaco was very happy to see him alive and well. "Boy, I say I coming to take refuge by you and Sisserou, but here worse than by me. You mean Maria pass here too?"

Manicou was grief stricken "Yes. And some people come, and they take Sisserou and go with him."

"How you mean take?" asked Jaco.

"All I know they come with a patchay fruits and nuts in a shiny cage. Time I run up, I see them going," whimpered Manicou.

Jaco found this strange, because his friend Sisserou generally avoided contact with people. He took it upon himself to find out what had happened to his good friend. He began to ask Manicou specific questions. "So which way they go with him?" he asked.

Manicou, who was busy gathering exposed snails, replied, "De road dat going to town." His overfilled mouth dripped fluids.

This territory was unknown to Jaco, but his concern for his friend gave him courage and motivation to make the journey. Manicou knew the way quite well because he often travelled long distances late at night in search of food. The two decided to execute a rescue mission with Manicou the expert tracker and Jaco the brains of the outfit. And so began the journey into the unknown.

The long twisting of road which was quite visible through the stripped foliage seemed to enjoy disappearing through endless recurring rubble. At an area called Red Gully, the entire track was covered by a monumental landslide.

"Well, it looks like we have to go back," grumbled Manicou as he shook off some mud from his tail. "Me self doh like dem la-boo business there."

Jaco was too busy looking for clues to listen to Manicou's concern. He noticed a few footprints leading over the landslide and was ecstatic.

"Boy, look there dem man pass, wii," he said as he pointed the way.

"How we getting over dat?" asked Manicou. "And I just clean my fur!"

Fortunately, Jaco was an expert at beak and claw acrobatics. He spun and tumbled his way over the rubble. Manicou followed closely behind, complaining about the sticky mud between his toes. They encountered quite a few dead animals beyond the obstacle. Their deaths saddened Jaco to the point that he almost felt like giving up. He was hungry, and his little feet were numb, but there were no fruits or seeds in sight—nothing but death and debris. There wasn't any time to sit and rest, either. They had no choice but to press on. It sickened him when he observed that Manicou was picking off small dead animals and eating them.

"Boy, what you doing there? You sick, man?" shouted Jaco.

"Free food," mumbled Manicou, his mouth full of spoilt flesh.

He tried to convince Jaco to do the same in order to gain strength, but the prince would have nothing to do with eating rotting meat. Sighing, Jaco drank a bit of water from an overflowing ravine and continued to waddle on his way. Battered and weak, he was only fuelled by the hope of finding his dear friend Sisserou alive.

The two animals traversed the demolished environment until they arrived on the west coast of the island. There was still no sight of Sisserou or the people who had taken him. In fact, there weren't any people visible at all. Suddenly a large, ferocious dog came at them from the basement of a toppled house.

"Run Jaco!" shouted Manicou as he dove into a clutch of shrubs.

Jaco took off in the opposite direction as fast as his short legs could carry him, but he had very little energy left. He collapsed into an open drain.

Jaco awoke the next day, to find two other birds that looked identical to him staring down from an overhead perch. Confused, he soon realised that he was trapped inside a large cage. Still unable to fly, Jaco attempted to conceal himself near a plant on the floor. He called out to the other parrots.

"Hey, padnas. Where I be there, nuh? All you see Sisserou around?"

But they never responded. They monitored him closely as they whispered to each other. The bewildered Prince Jaco called for help as he frantically sought a way out of the cage. This once glorious parrot had become a prisoner of fate in a steel enclosure. The others didn't seem to care, because they were regularly fed and watered by people. Prince Jaco, on the other hand, was a free-spirited bird and could not adjust to this confined life. He questioned everyone who went by as to where Sisserou might be, but he got no answers.

Trust no one, he told himself. He suspected that the other parrots and the human caretakers might all be in on it. He kept on guard for any available loopholes that could aid in his escape.

After a few months, the natural environment of the island began to restore itself. Jaco's beautiful feathers reclaimed their glory, but to no avail—he remained a shadow of his former self. Day after day, Jaco stared mindlessly as people came and went. He performed beak and claw acrobatics around his cage to keep from completely losing his mind. No longer speaking, the Prince of Gossip had ceased all communication with others because this life of incarceration was too much. Some people heard sadness in the sounds made by Prince Jaco as he mourned for his lost friends, but they couldn't comprehend the reason.

One morning at regular feeding time, the prince was found lying motionless inside of his cage. Distraught, the keepers ran to his aid in fear of the worst. The sound of rusted gate hinges alerted him as he was lifted off the cold floor, but he was so weak that he couldn't hold his head upright as the keepers placed him on a nearby table for inspection. One deep breath after another, he struggled to recover. Discerning that he may have not been eating properly, the keepers tried to manually feed him. This was it! Finally, his chance to escape! Jaco made a mad dash for the open gate. He smiled as a feeling of freedom overtook him. That was when he realised that his home cage had been inside of a much larger cage all along.

"Tough luck Jaco. Maybe next time," called one of the keepers. The distraught jail breaker once again collapsed, stung by disbelief and disappointment.


Jaco never found Sisserou. It wasn't clear whether Manicou had escaped the dog that night, so he was added to the long list of uncertainties in his mind. As he continues to mentally engineer escape plans, Jaco remains bitter that he never got to meet that savage visitor, Maria. He has such a beak full that he intends to dump on her unruly head—she ruined his home, cost him a dear friend, and changed his life forever.

To date, Prince Jaco remains at the Botanic Gardens where he has adapted to entertaining visitors. But sadly, they are all oblivious as to who he truly is. Yeah, man. Jaco is a prince who owns an airport and a mountain. He's an adventurer and the master of gossip, not a joker trained as sideshow entertainment for tourists.

# That Night

A true-life recount of the night of Hurricane Maria by 12-year-old Princess

*Wam! Bang! Clatter!*

"What was that?" I asked with apprehension.

"The dogs' plates were just blown into the back sink" answered my excited little brother, Bob, as he stood looking out of the living room window.

"Here we go again," whispered Grandma Mary.

*Screech, Screech, crash!*

Whispers, my tiger striped cat, let out a loud meow as he wisely made a hasty exit.

"So it has really started," moaned Grandpa. He walked towards his wife.

"What has started?" asked Grandma.

"The hurricane," said Grandpa.

"Alan James Joakim-Stoute, please do not say that. The weatherman clearly stated less than an hour ago, that the hurricane is not expected until 8pm. Now it is only half past 6," said Grandma in a firm voice.

"Look here, Mary Pamela Jones-Stoute," Grandpa answered. "It has started."

*Crick, crick, crash!*

"What! A branch with ripe juicy mangoes just broke off from my mango tree," wailed Bob.

"Oh no," bellowed Grandma. She hugged herself with both hands. "I remember 1979, and I don't want to ever go through that again, no way not at all."

I sat on the blue and gold living room couch and listened to my grandparents who were undoubtedly going to talk about Hurricane David. I momentarily ignored the

SARAH ABRAHAM is a primary school principal with three decades of experience as a classroom teacher. A strong believer in the power of words, she specialises in literacy and regularly conducts training sessions with teachers, parents, and students. She enjoys a good book but also loves sea and river bathing in the refreshing waters of her native Dominica.

storm building up outside and listened to the exchange between them. My romantically-inclined grandfather sat on the sofa and reminded his dear wife that he was on his way to visit her on the day that David inflicted his rage on Dominica.

"Oh yes," beamed Grandmother. She reached for her husband's hands. "I was so excited that you were coming for a visit that I got up early that morning to complete all my chores."

"You sure mister coming all that way from Roseau to Delices to visit you in this weather?" my mother had asked.

"Yes, Mama. He will come because he loves me," I boasted. "Soon you will meet my handsome, brave policeman beau."

"Foolish girl," she said and walked away.

I looked at my grandmother's brightly lit face as she spoke about my young grandfather and tried to imagine how she felt on that day while waiting for him to show up.

Grandfather smiled as he looked lovingly at her and planted a kiss on her forehead. "That was the roughest and best day of my life."

"Here is the latest update on Hurricane Maria," said the weatherman on the television.

All eyes in the room turned towards the huge TV that hung on the wall.

"So we will get a direct hit," murmured Grandfather.

"It's just a Category 1 hurricane," I reminded him.

He shrugged then stared ahead. I knew he was thinking about the mighty Hurricane David again. Growing up with my caring grandparents, I had heard many stories about Hurricane David. I earnestly prayed that this Hurricane Maria would not be as severe as David was.

I rose from my comfortable seat and looked outside. The little drizzles had suddenly become a torrential downpour. The wind was picking up, and the trees were dancing like drunken men.

"Do you think our newly repaired roof will go?" asked my brother Bob anxiously.

"It better not!" exclaimed Grandfather. "I just spent an arm and a leg to replace it less than a year ago."

Suddenly the power went out, and we were plunged into darkness. I shivered involuntarily, and then heard my grandmother groan from across the room.

"Where is the torchlight?" asked Grandfather.

"Under your chair," replied Grandmother.

"There is also a small one under your chair, Princess," said Grandma.

I searched under my chair and located the torch.

"I think we should all go into the master bedroom to ride out this hurricane," Grandfather said.

We all stood as Grandfather led the way, followed by my grandmother, Bob, and me.

We were hardly seated on the huge, king size bed when we heard a loud bang.

"What was that?" screamed my grandmother.

"I'm not sure," said my grandfather.

"I will go and see," I bravely proclaimed.

"Oh no, don't go," pleaded Grandmother. She grabbed my arm.

"I have my torchlight, so it will be alright," I said as I escaped from her grasp.

"Can I come with you?" asked Bob.

"No, stay with Grandma and Grandpa. I won't be long," I replied.

With the torch on, I made my way to where I thought the noise came from. I stood in amazement as I looked at Bob's mango tree enjoying itself inside our living room. It looked so funny hanging there between the broken glass windows. The rain was pouring into the room through the panes. I pinched myself to ensure that I was really seeing this in real life and it was not a dream.

At that moment a blinding light entered the room followed by a loud clap of thunder. I screamed and ran back as fast as a cheetah into the bedroom.

"What happened?" asked Grandfather.

"Our mango tree fell onto the windows and now is in the living room," I said.

On hearing that, my grandmother began to cry.

"Don't cry, Mary," said my grandfather. He drew his wife towards him and hugged her.

"Can I go and see?" asked my brother.

"No!" we all shouted together.

*Ripppp, rippp, whoosh!* Off flew a sheet of galvanise from over our head.

"Oh no," I lamented. I reached out and held Bob's cold hands.

"Quick, quick into the closet!" shouted Grandpa as he pushed Grandma ahead. "You too, Princess. Get in."

"What about you, Alan?" wailed Grandmother.

Before he could answer Bob squeezed his way through and knelt on the floor between Grandma and me in the closet.

*Grrrr, grrrr, whoosh!* Off went another sheet of galvanise.

Grandma shrieked, "Alan, where are you?"

"Right here," said Grandpa holding on to the door while trying to fit into the overcrowded closet.

I shone the flashlight into the open space left by the departed sheets of galvanised. All I could see was darkness. All types of noises were heard around us as more of our roof made its untimely departure. It was as if a crane and a tractor were at work over our heads.

"I thought you said our roof would not go because you spent an arm and a leg to replace it less than a year ago, Grandpa," said Bob.

Boom, wam, bang, crash! was heard instead of Grandpa's answer to Bob's question.

"My 72-inch flat-screen TV your father sent for us just fell," sobbed Granny.

"You can't worry about that now, Mary," Grandpa told Grandma.

*Thump.* Something landed on the bed. We all screamed.

"Alan, what landed on the bed?" whispered my grandmother.

*Creak, screech, thud, crash!*

"God help us," cried Grandma.

"Is the house breaking up, Grandpa?" asked Bob.

"*Plop, chink, Plop, plop, clang, splash!* A river of water greeted us as more of the galvanise sheets made their exit.

"I want my mother," wailed Bob.

"God has not given us a spirit of fear," whimpered Grandmother.

"That's right, Mary, God has not given us a spirit of fear," said my grandfather. "Repeat after me everyone. 'God has not given us a spirit of fear!'"

*Hiss, sniff, boo, bleep ra ta ta ta bang!* The entire house vibrated as something exploded nearby. "God has not given us a spirit of fear!" I shouted.

*Swish, sizzle, blare, boom!* The closet swung from side to side. Grandma collapsed into Grandpa's back.

"My head," moaned Bob as Grandpa's knees buckled under Grandma's weight and she toppled onto him.

"Gentle, my love, my dove, my everything, can you hear me?" asked Grandfather.

I could feel something moving in my stomach, a bitter taste came in my mouth and my chest hurt. The flashlight fell from my hand. *Thump.* "Boohoo, sniff, sniff." The sounds came from the floor near my feet.

"I'm afraid. My head hurts. I can't breathe. I'm dying," sobbed Bob.

My grandfather prayed. "Heavenly Father give me strength, I need you right now."

"Put your hands in the air, put your hands in the air." The tune jingled from my pocket.

"Princess, answer your phone," said Grandfather.

"My phone?" I asked in a puzzled voice.

"Yes, it's in your pocket. Reach for it."

Before I could move, I felt a hand reaching into my pocket.

"Hello. Hello," Bob said. "Hello, Daddy. Yes, I can hear you."

"Put the phone on speaker, Bob," ordered Grandpa.

"Is everyone alright?" I heard my father's voice from the phone.

"Yes, we are alright," shouted Grandpa.

"No, we are not!" I exclaimed

"My head hurts, and Grandma is dead," whimpered Bob

"The TV, the TV," whispered Grandma. "Save the TV!"

"She is alive! Daddy, Grandma is alive!" yelled Bob into the phone.

*Bump, clip, clop, clunk, crash.* Something fell close to the closet.

"Princess, hello! Can you hear me? Maria is now a Category 5 hurricane. You all need to get downstairs!"

"There is no such thing as a Category 5 hurricane, son," said Grandpa.

"Can't be," cried Grandma.

"Sweet Jesus," I whispered in a panicked voice when the light went off on the phone.

"Your phone just died, Princess," Bob said angrily. "Why you were WhatsApping on it all afternoon?"

"Listen," I said. "It's over."

"Oh no it's not. The eye is just passing now," said Grandfather.

"Let's run downstairs," shouted Bob.

"Your flashlight, Princess. I found it," he said. He turned it on and immediately stumbled into the heavy chest of drawers located directly in front of us.

"How did that get there?" asked Bob.

"Can you stand for a minute, Mary? I need to shift that chest," said Grandfather.

"I'll help," I said.

"Me too," yelled Bob.

"Quickly then, all of you. We don't have a lot of time before the hurricane starts again," said Grandpa.

"Ok, one, two, three, push," I said.

Grandma prayed, "Give them strength, heavenly father."

"Give Grandma the torch, Bob, so that you can use your both hands," I said.

"Rocks you have it that, man?" asked Grandpa as we tried pushing.

The room was suddenly brightly lit by a flash of lightning. A crack of thunder that shook the house followed it.

"Push, push!" screamed Grandpa.

We all pushed, even Grandma.

"Come on you all. Let's try to squeeze our way out now!"

*Thump!* Bob had bumped into something.

"Grandma, give me the light," I shouted.

The light from the touch landed on a tall white mountain of the fridge directly in front of us. My heart fell as I felt water stinging my skin.

Grandpa said, "The fridge has wheels, so let's try pushing it out of the way."

There was a sound like a gigantic bonfire going off. *Boom, crack, crash.*

"Mary, give me your hand. We have to get downstairs now," instructed Grandfather.

We hurriedly made our way through the debris which was once our precious possessions. We got battered by rain and almost knocked over by the fierce winds that were picking up around us, but we kept going.

Finally, we were downstairs. Without warning, *Slosh, splat, splash*, could be heard as we stepped into a deep pool of water.

"Is now we drown," lamented Grandma.

"Out of the frying pan into the fire," I said dejectedly.

"Princess, this is not funny," said Bob while trying to wade through the water.

"Relax and breathe, Princess," said Grandfather.

"If I breathe, I will drown," I said.

"Climb onto that table, Princess and Bob," said Grandma.

"At least I can't see the sky over my head anymore," said Grandpa.

"This is not going well," said Bob as he tried to scramble up.

I helped him onto the table, but Grandma couldn't make it.

"Come and stand on this black box, my love," Grandfather said to his wife.

"Oh no. There goes our light," I cried as the flashlight fell and disappeared into the water.

"Can this get worse?" I asked and was quickly answered by a flash of lightning and a blast of thunder.

"Alan, I'm falling off this box," wailed Grandma.

"Hold on tightly to Grandpa, Grandma," Bob shouted. "I am coming to save you."

"Just keep your troublesome backside on this table, little boy," I said crossly.

"Princess, what is wrong with you?" asked Grandma.

"I wish my parents were here. I'm so sick and tired of this blasted hurricane."

*Wham, crash!* A window broke next to me, and rain gushed in drenching me all over. I felt a weight descend on my shoulders and miraculously fell asleep.

"Princess, Princess, Princess!" I heard my name being called from a distance.

"Princess, wake up. It's over." I opened my eyes and looked into the concerned face of my brother.

"It's really over?" I asked doubtfully. "Or is the worst just about to begin?"

# Madame Poverty

Magdalene sits on her expansive veranda with her dog at her feet. Sipping wine for courage, she toys with the remote control that opens and closes the gate at the end of the driveway. She used to imagine the ornamental iron had the power to keep her locked inside forever, but now she feels it's time to take control of her destiny. What's the point in living in a prison of your own creation when freedom awaits you? Magdalene removes her velvet slippers. "Open Sesame!" she commands. The identical halves of the monogrammed gate swing wide. Emboldened, she marches down the road with Stella, her loyal Doberman, leading the way. It feels good to be barefoot in the rain, as if she's a carefree child again. But Magdalene is aware that she's no longer young, and, according to the villagers, 'Old is something to throw.'

When they reach the chain link fence that marks the boundary of the property, dog and mistress peer into the darkening ravine. Dense foliage shrouds the banks of a river on the other side. Mist rises from a waterfall as it plunges over the edge of a cliff into a deep, green pool. The river flows obediently downhill from there, as if unable to resist. Magdalene spies the seaside village of Poverty, the place where she was born, nestled far below. In her muddled mind, it beckons like a magnet, an unspoiled sanctuary where true happiness might still be possible. The sun sets over the bay while she ponders her next move. They say all rivers run to the sea, so why shouldn't she?

KRISTINE SIMELDA, co-founder of Waitukubuli Writers, has been a citizen of Dominica since 1995. Her short fiction has appeared in many regional and international journals, and her imprint, River Ridge Press Dominica, has self-published three adult novels and a novella for young adults. Her website is www.kristinesimelda.wordpress.com

Surveying the landscape of her homeland earlier that morning, Magdalene had been unimpressed by the island's beauty. The glorious sunrise that highlighted the hills failed to lift her spirits, nor was she cheered by the pink clouds that danced around the mountaintops. She sucked her teeth when it started to rain, turned her back as a double rainbow arced over the valley. Returning after years overseas, she had half-hoped to slip back into the light-hearted lifestyle she had left behind. But she had been sorely disappointed. Now she needed to figure a way out of this cold-blooded place called Morne Prosper, her current residence, a way to escape from the sense of blatant rejection that surrounded it.

Stella rested her head on her paws as if she too was bored with the scenery. Stroking the dog's silky ears, Magdalene remembered what had compelled her to trade what was warm and familiar for that which was cold and uncaring in the first place.

"Andreas," she said. "If not for Andreas, I might have settled down among friends and family. Who knows? Loving children and grandchildren could have blessed me in my old age instead of this perpetual curse of estrangement. Why did I have to abandon everything to follow a man who cared only for himself? Why did I have to reach for the stars?"

Immune to disagreeable memories, Stella thumped her amputated tail. Magdalene ignored her. She wasn't seeking the dog's opinion; she already knew the answer to her own question. Like most young people on the island, she had simply wanted to escape. Not just from the village of Poverty, but from the paralysing state of affairs that plagued islanders' lives in general. Young Maggie dreamed of being rich and famous, but Magdalene, as Andreas had insisted on calling her, now realised that monetary and spiritual poverty were two separate conditions. Even though her family had been poor, she was happy as a child. Spiritual poverty was something else entirely. It was the illness that had infected her while she was away and followed her back home like a malignant shadow. *Élas.* Her years overseas with Andreas had effectively ruined her health and sealed her heart against the possibility of happy endings.

Magdalene's caretaker, Yvonne, interrupted her unpleasant thoughts when she brought tea and some digestive biscuits arranged on a silver tray. "Morning, Madame. How was your sleep?"

"Nonexistent," she said, "but thanks for asking."

"Sorry to hear that," said Yvonne. She poured, added two cubes of white sugar just the way she knew Madame enjoyed it, and disappeared.

Magdalene's hands shook as she sipped the oversweet liquid; the porcelain cup rattled in its saucer when she replaced it. If only she could convince Yvonne to live in instead of returning to her extended family each afternoon. Then maybe she wouldn't feel so deserted. She remembered how, as girls, she and her best friend Yvonne had drunk tea made from all sorts of wild bush at pretend tea parties. But the legend who changed her name from Maggie to Magdalene had left ordinary people like Yvonne behind.

Maggie had been born the last of six children, and she was the only girl to boot. Things were hard in the village of Poverty, her birthplace by the sea. With no running water in the house, no fridge, and only a coal pot for cooking food, the maintenance of her family's meagre existence was a never-ending chore. There were buckets to carry, wood to collect, fish to clean, and animals to tend. Still, the trade winds were fresh, the sea crystal clear, and she was free to dream to her heart's content. Maggie was also fortunate in other ways. On an island where skin colour and hair texture determined social class, she was blessed with a light complexion and wavy locks. She had always wondered how this was possible. Both of her parents were dark, as were the rest of her close relatives. She knew her father had outside women, so why couldn't Mama have outside men?

"How come my skin so bright and my hair so smooth?" Maggie asked.

"Just be grateful, child," said her mother.

"But the kids in the village are always teasing me. They say my father must be a white man, maybe that skinny priest who left the village right after my First Communion."

Her mother pretended to be shocked. "Maggie! How you can talk such nonsense?"

"Sorry, I thought you liked him," she said sheepishly.

"Well, whatever you do, don't mention him in front of your father."

Another blessing materialised in the form of public education. Although her father protested that schooling only made women difficult to handle, her mother had argued that Maggie deserved a chance at a better life. She learned to read and write, decipher a bit of math, and digested the Eurocentric version of colonial history that was currently in favour.

The third windfall came from abroad. From the time she was small, Maggie had been taught what was foreign was more precious than what was local. Her mother added tinned vegetables and potted meat to enhance the flavour of provisions that came straight from the rich volcanic soil. She considered imported codfish and pickled mackerel, even of poor quality, superior to the fresh tuna that her father caught in the sea. At Christmastime, Mama purchased candied fruit of unnatural colour to put in her baking as opposed to the more nutritious coconut rough cakes they ate every day. So when Andreas, a white photographer from overseas, chose Maggie for a spread in his fashionable travel magazine, she was extremely flattered.

"You're a beautiful girl with a beautiful smile," he said, winking.

The copies of the magazine Andreas sent down were of professional quality and showcased Maggie's tall, shapely body set against glistening Caribbean scenery. But she kept the pictures hidden—she knew how vindictive village girls could be, and she didn't want rude boys pestering her. "I'm saving myself for the white man," Maggie whispered to Yvonne.

When the free schooling ran out, Maggie took a job as a housekeeper at a tourist villa up the coast. It wasn't long before the expat owner noticed her pretty face and tempting figure. Late one night, while she was washing glasses in the beach bar, he crept up behind her. "Hold still, my dear," he said, wheezing. Maggie managed to wriggle free, but she knew it was just a matter of time until he got his way.


At lunchtime, Magdalene worked a crossword puzzle while she waited for Yvonne to bring her salad and diet soda. She had stopped eating starchy island food years ago when she started modelling. "What was it we used to say in the dressing room before a major fashion show?" she asked her caretaker.

Yvonne, who bore the plumpness of someone who ate whatever they wanted whenever they were hungry, shrugged. "I wouldn't know, Madame."

"A woman can never be rich or thin enough," Magdalene said, chewing the bitter greens. But although she was elegantly slim and surrounded by expensive things, she ached with loneliness. "If it wasn't for Stella, I wouldn't have a friend in the world," she said, sighing.

Being intimate with the hotelier substantially increased Maggie's pocketbook, wardrobe, and sexual prowess. When the villa sold, she moved on to a job in a trendy boutique in town. The men who came in to shop for their girlfriends had money, and she wasn't above sleeping with them when there was a dress or pair of shoes that she wanted for herself. Besides, her mama was sick, and she needed extra money to help with her doctor bills.

"How about sharing some of that sugar?" the men said, grinning.

Fifty Eastern Caribbean dollars had been her opening price. All she had to do was play nice. After it was finished, they left her alone in a room with hot water in the shower and a clean, comfortable bed.

One Friday evening after work, while Maggie was hanging around a portside bar with her friend Yvonne, three flush-looking tourists came in. They seemed friendly enough and bought several rounds of drinks before inviting the young women aboard their sailboat.

Yvonne declined. "Come on, girl. Time to go on home," she said.

Maggie, who thought she knew everything about the ways of the world, accepted the tourists' invitation. The men plied her with alcohol spiked with drugs to the point of blind capitulation. When she woke up, she was slumped on a bench beside the harbour. The boat was gone, and she was extremely sore all over. She hobbled back to the shack where she and Yvonne lived during the week, undressed, and examined herself in the mirror. Her face was unmarked, but bruises and welts were beginning to form on her wrists and the insides of her thighs.

She dabbed at her wounds with antiseptic. "How could I have been so stupid?" Humiliated, she dropped her rumpled dress and soiled underwear into a plastic bag and hid them in the trash. Then she showered, lathering up several times, and crawled onto her narrow bunk. As night-time wrapped itself around her, Maggie felt buried alive under a burden of guilt and shame. She pulled the sheets up tight, closed her eyes, and wept.

Yvonne, bearing the required pot of afternoon tea plus trimmings, poured and disappeared again. Magdalene fed the biscuits to the dog while she recalled what happened next. Andreas had rematerialised, as if by magic, to take her away. She had gone with him eagerly, traded her friends, family, and island culture for icons she believed to be much more significant: a white man, and a spread in a glossy magazine. But her life overseas got off to a rocky start.

"Andreas, I have something to tell you."

"What is it, my dear?"

"I'm pregnant," she whispered, "from the time with the tourists on the boat."

"And I'm late for the office," he said, scowling. "Get rid of it!"

Andreas paid for the abortion, set her up in her own flat, and then transformed her into Magdalene, the Caribbean supermodel. As far as the public was concerned, they were an ideal couple, but in private, his idea of devotion was much more liberal than hers. His string of lightly disguised affairs with both men and women shattered her pride and broke her heart. She was so dismayed that she secretly plotted to have another baby, hoping a child would bind Andreas to her forever. But as the years rolled by, her dream of raising a family with the only man she had ever loved evaporated right along with her self-esteem.

"People like us weren't meant to have children," Andreas said bluntly.

"What about adoption?" she asked.

He rolled his eyes. "We're too busy for something as mundane as that."

From that moment on, her life became a meaningless charade. She was cross. She was depressed. She was remote. Yet she never once wrote or phoned those she had left behind—the hurt in her heart was too heavy to share with Mama, who was already sick, or even with her best chum Yvonne. Years passed as she kept her pain hidden behind extravagant hairstyles, carefully applied makeup, and designer clothes; she used the fashion runway as a ruse to cover up her sense of isolation.

Eventually Magdalene retired from modelling and took over as editor of the magazine. Meanwhile, Andreas continued his bi-sexual escapades. When he died in the bed of his last lover, Magdalene had him cremated and handed his ashes over to his paramour. All she had left of him were his photographs, mostly of herself, which lingered like testaments to her faded beauty. But lately they had begun to look counterfeit in her eyes, just like her life with the man who had taken them.

With Andreas gone, Magdalene was free to return to the island. What she failed to realise was that it was too late to salvage any sense of belonging.

Her parents were both dead, and her brothers were scattered. People that she had once considered friends shunned her. In islanders' eyes, she was too proud of her lofty mansion, surrounded as it was by high fence and forbidding gates. It vexed them when she boasted she could see the four corners of the island right down to the sea without leaving her veranda. They were worried that she could make out the rusty tin roofs of the village of Poverty, as if she had risen above the place of her birth and its lowly inhabitants.

"*Gadé* Madame Poverty," they teased behind her back. "She likes to play big, but see how small she get. *Humph*. All that time she gone, we never heard a peep. What she want with us now?"

So Magdalene, surrounded by mounds of pretentious things she had collected and shipped down in a metal container at great expense, still felt impoverished. She had come home, yes, but Morne Prosper, with its stunning view and lavish furnishings, made her feel as if she was a stranger in a foreign land. She had money, but all the money in the world couldn't buy back Yvonne's friendship or restore her enthusiasm for living. Maggie the island girl aimed for the stars, but rich and famous Magdalene had fallen short of grace.

Yvonne counts out Madam's meds and covers her supper on the stove before leaving. Magdalene sniffs at the food, downs the pills with a glass of wine, and then wanders out into the rain with Stella by her side. Standing at the end of the driveway with her wig soaked and her dressing gown plastered to her fragile frame, she peers into oblivion. So. It has come down to this—a shrivelled up old woman, whose only friend is a dog, has returned to a place that no longer wants her. Stella's sharp eyes spot an agouti scurrying through the bush, but she is too well behaved to go after it. She whines in apprehension as Magdalene clutches at the fence and chokes back tears.

It would be easy enough to find a way around and step over the edge. She could spread imaginary wings and glide over the waterfall. She could fly along the river as it wound its way down the ravine, and then soar with the seabirds that cruised high above the village of Poverty. But in her heart Magdalene knows it would be different. Gravity would inevitably take over, bones would break, and blood would flow. Most probably, she would lie undetected on the tangled path and suffer a hideous, drawn-out death before anyone noticed she was missing

Magdalene sighs and wipes her nose on her sleeve. "And who would take care of dear Stella after I'm gone?" The dog pricks her ears when she hears her name. She realises Stella's heart would be broken if she was left behind, and, having been abandoned herself, she can't bear the thought. When Stella pushes her muzzle into her hand, Magdalene bends down and kisses the top of her head. "I love you," she says, sniffing.

The dog is suddenly playful. She tugs at the hem of the dressing gown as if to lead her mistress back to the house. Magdalene takes one last look at the far-off village of Poverty, bathed as it is in the lingering light of a colourful Caribbean sunset, and pitches her empty wine glass over the fence. "Come on, girl. Time to go on home."

# Ma And I

When the letter arrived from Dominica, it took me two days to summon the courage to open it. It had been over ten years since I'd received a letter from home, and I was afraid of whatever information this one contained. Most likely the news was bad. Very bad.

I left Dominica in the late 70s when I was sixteen. It was hard for Ma since I was her only child. But she wanted the best for me, wanted me to seek my fortunes in places where opportunities were aplenty.

I chose the French island of Marie-Galante simply because it was close by, right across the channel, and I joined a wave of young Dominicans going to work on sugar plantations there.

For months before my departure, Ma worked hard weaving baskets and cultivating all kinds of crops to sell to make sure I had the money I needed.

In the dead of night, I took a small boat loaded with other eager young men and slipped unseen to Marie-Galante. I was lucky. I got a job the next day on a big sugar plantation and settled down to work. The estate owner was impressed and soon placed me in charge of a group of men on the plantation.

Those days were happy days. I wrote home every week, and Ma responded in kind. I looked forward to these correspondences because I missed her dearly. But over time my letter-writing habit changed. I began writing once a month, then once every six months, and finally once a year. Eventually I stopped.

Now, over ten years later, I had received a letter from

ROY SANFORD was born in the Kalinago Territory in Dominica. He was a journalist at the Jamaica Gleaner for many years and editor of Dominica News on Line. A lover of folklore, he is the author of *Three Nights Later, the Soukouyan on the Roof and Other Stories*. He is married and father to one son.

Dominica that was not in Ma's handwriting. For two days, I was afraid of the tidings it bore.

So I hid the letter underneath a mattress and went along my normal duties, but I could not concentrate. I felt ashamed, guilty, and regretful. Receipt of the letter jerked me into the stark realisation that I had abandoned my mother, the woman who worked so hard to get me going in life.

I remembered Ma once told me that I would forget her one day. I swore such a day would never come to pass. But she only laughed, and not out of amusement.

I was sweating profusely when I finally pulled the letter from underneath the mattress. It felt heavy. With trembling hands, I opened it carefully, as if I was afraid a slight mistake might affect its contents.

The letter was written by my niece, Marvella, and it was over a month old. My heart sank. The news was indeed bad. Ma was gravely ill and had been asking for me. She said she wanted to see me at all costs.

It took my brain about a minute to digest the information.

I knew I had to go to Dominica, and fast. But that was going to be a daunting task. My Dominican passport had expired some years ago, and I had no French documents. The small boats that used to sneak across the channel from Dominica to Marie-Galante had all but ceased operations. Only an occasional one loaded with marijuana and other contraband now attempted the journey.

After reading the letter, I headed down to the beach. I thought I might be lucky enough to get some information about making the stealthy trip home. Across the sea, Dominica lay like a huge whale. Every urge in me wanted to hurl myself into the water and swim across.

A week later, I found a boat and once again in the dead of night, like so many years ago, I made my way back across to the island where I was born.

I arrived in Dominica at around 10:00 pm at Anse de Mai, where I hired a bus home. It was 11:30 when I finally arrived. Everything seemed surreal, like I was in a dream. After all, it had been a decade since I left.

I walked up the dark path towards our house. There was a solitary light coming from the living room, but otherwise the structure where I grew up was enveloped by darkness. Even so, it appeared bigger and more imposing than I remembered.

I walked to the door, but I was unsure of what to do. Should I knock? Wouldn't I disturb those inside? After all, it was very late.

To my surprise, the door was slightly ajar. It groaned as I gently pushed it open and peered inside.

The smell of stale air mixed with Vicks VapoRub®, Alcalado®, and bush medicine greeted my nostrils. On the table, a kerosene lamp burnt low. Seated on a rocking chair in the far corner with its back towards me was a dark, huddled figure. Although the light was poor, I recognised my mother instantly.

I stepped inside. Although the house was closed, I felt suddenly cold. I shivered. A tingling sensation ran up and down my spine. I felt as if the earth beneath me was swinging to the left and then swinging to the right. I grabbed the door to maintain my balance.

*I must be tired*, I thought to myself. It had been a long day of travel. I had left my home in Marie-Galante early that morning and gone to the beach to await the boat. It came long after night had fallen. The journey itself was nerve wracking because the French and Dominican coast guards plied the waters on an ever-constant vigil for smugglers. A few times during the trip, the captain killed the engines, and we sat in silence while he peered through the darkness. I could not wait to get to Dominica.

Still holding on to the door, I quickly regained my senses. I could see my mother from where I was standing, but it appeared as if a great chasm, which I could never cross, existed between us.

A wave of emotions swept over me, but I didn't know what to do. Should I go over and hug my mother? Should I keep my distance since she was gravely ill? What was she suffering from, anyway? Marvella never revealed Ma's illness in her letter.

To my surprise, as if reading my mind, Ma was the first to speak, "De doctor say doh come close to me. I might give you de cold."

Her voice sounded strange, different from how I remembered it, but I was glad the initial awkward moment was over.

"I get the letter Marvella send, Ma," I said searching for something to start a conversation.

I was expecting an angry outburst from her for abandoning her all those years. From childhood I knew that Ma spoke her mind freely, and she told you whatever she was thinking. "I doh putting hot food in my mouth to tell you what I have to tell you eh," she used to say.

Then she coughed, a dry, metallic cough.

I was worried by the sound of the cough, but I felt relieved that the ice that formed over the years was beginning to melt away.

But I was still standing near the door, my luggage at my feet, unsure of what to do next.

Then again, as if reading my mind, Ma said, "You can take your things in your room."

*My room?*

When I left Dominica, our house had one bed-room and Ma slept in it, while I slept on a foam mattress on the floor in the living room. I didn't know Ma had built a room for me, and I felt more guilty than ever.

As if reading my mind, she said, "It's ok. Your uncle built it when you was away."

She pointed to the room.

"It have a candle on the table by the window," Ma said.

The door creaked as I opened it. The smell of stale air hung heavily in the room as if no one had entered it in a long time. My first instinct was to find my way to the window and open it to let in some fresh air.

I dropped my luggage and groped my way in the darkness to the window. Suddenly I felt as if someone standing next to me. I automatically reached out, hoping to touch whoever it was, but only empty space met my hands.

Confused, I froze.

"Ma?" I whispered, more by instinct than anything else.

There was no response, and the strange sensation did not go away.

"Ma?" I repeated peering through the darkness. But only silence answered me.

I felt my head growing big. I felt weak as I groped shivering in the dark, trying to find something to lean on.

Ma's voice wafted in. "You tired, man. You had a long day."

I jumped, and I realised I was sweating.

Relief flowed over me when I managed to locate a box of matches on the window ledge.

The light revealed a neat but small room, and the sensation that someone else was in there with me, evaporated.

There was a bed with a small table beside it. Then I saw something that raised goosebumps all over me. A homemade oil lamp was on it. I remembered as a child that they were made only when people died and were kept burning nonstop for nine nights after death. I dreaded these lamps because of their association with death. I wondered what one was doing in here.

But before I could think any further, Ma's voice flowed in again, "Marvella 'range your bed for you, eh."

"Yes, Ma," I said squeakily.

When I went to the window with the intention of opening it, I heard Ma's voice again. "De doctor say we have to keep the window close or de cold will not get better."

I abandoned the window. In the middle of the bed was a white pillow. When I touched it, I realised it was covered with a thin layer of dust and was heavy as a stone. I could not lift it up.

I was baffled, and for the second time that night, I felt my head growing. I began feeling drowsy, and for a split second, I lost the sense of reality.

I jumped at the sound of Ma's voice. "Is tired you tired, man. You had a long day, you know."

I grabbed the pillow, determined to lift it, and this time it was light as a feather. *This is weird*, I thought to myself. *I've had many inexplicable feelings since entering the house. Am I really that tired?*

I placed the pillow at the top of the bed and went back to the living room.

I sat heavily on a chair, ready to discuss with Ma the sickness that was afflicting her and to explore ways to combat it.

As I began speaking, Ma interrupted me.

"It have food in de kitchen, you know," she said. She coughed again. "Marvella cook food this afternoon." She stopped and added, "Élas, if it wasn't for Marvella, I doh know what I would do, eh. Although she married and have her house, she do everything for me."

Her last words struck me hard, and guilt swept over me. *What did I do to my mother?* I thought to myself.

Ma appeared to be reading my thoughts once again.

"But doh worry your head, man. Marvella is family, eh," she said.

I could not stay silent anymore. "But Ma," I said. "Every time I think of something, it look like you know what I thinking and you know what I going to say."

A period of uncomfortable silence followed. From where I was sitting, I could not see her face. As a matter of fact, I hadn't seen her face since I arrived.

"It have food in the kitchen," she repeated. "Marvella cook food this afternoon."

In truth, I was not hungry. Food was not really on my mind. All I wanted was to get a some brighter light going in the house and have a chat with Ma.

She raised her hand. From childhood, I remembered whenever Ma raised her hand in such fashion, she meant business.

"It have food in de kitchen," she said assertively.

I followed the direction she pointed to the kitchen with a lit candle.

The kitchen was neat, and a gas stove had replaced the old wooden fireplace I remembered from long ago. On a table sat a covered dish. It contained fig and lamowee (green bananas and salt fish), which was my favourite.

"But Marvella not easy, eh, Ma," I said loud enough so she could hear. "She always know what I like."

Ma did not respond.

The sight of the food aroused hunger in me, but what was fig and lamowee without hot pepper? I remembered Ma could not eat her meals without hot pepper either, and that she grew her favourite type, *Bondah Ma Jack*, in the backyard.

"Ma, you have pepper there, nuh?" I asked.

There was no response.

"Ma, you have pepper there, nuh?" I repeated, louder.

Still no response.

Thinking that she had probably fallen asleep, I went to the window to open it for fresh air.

I was startled to see Ma outside in the darkness, close to what appeared to be a pepper tree.

"Ma," I yelled. "What are you doing outside there, nuh? You shouldn't be out at this time of the night, you know."

Fearing for her safety, I panicked and rushed from the kitchen to the living room. The rocking chair was empty. I ran outside. Ma was nowhere to be seen.

"Ma," I screamed.

I rushed to the back of the house but was greeted by only darkness.

"Ma."

Baffled, I raced back into the house. But as I was entering, my foot hit something, and I saw the floor rushing up to meet my face.

Then everything turned pitch black. I don't know how long I was out, but I was woken by the sound of a coconut broom in the yard.

When I opened my eyes, I was back in the room Ma said was mine. Sunlight streamed through a crack where the wall met the roof. I touched my face. It felt a bit swollen but was not painful.

The house itself was deathly silent, so I assumed Ma was still sleeping.

I opened the window quietly, afraid to awaken Ma. In the yard, Marvella was sweeping.

She was startled at the sound of the window being opened.

"Oh gosh, man, Heskeith, I didn't know you was there," she said when she realised it was me. "You nearly gave me a heart attack there, boy."

"I came home late last night," I said.

She dropped the coconut broom and moved closer to the window, cautiously as if I was some kind of jumbie or something. Her face showed a mixture of surprise and bewilderment.

"We didn't know you was coming, boy," she said.

"I wanted it to be a surprise," I lied.

"Well, you surprise me, man," Marvella responded. "And what happen to your face?"

"Nothing really," I said. "So you okay? Is a long time we doh see, eh."

She nodded saying, "I there, man. I come and sweep the yard, now and then. You know, keep the place clean."

"I sure Ma like that," I said.

Upon the mention of Ma, Marvella's countenance changed. She sat heavily on a stone near the window and began weeping, like a heartbroken child.

"What's the problem?" I asked quietly, still trying not to make enough noise to wake Ma.

"She was asking for you, she kept asking for you," Marvella wailed.

"Ok. Ok. I am here now," I responded.

"Even the day she died, Auntie was asking for you," Marvella said sobbing.

My heart leapt into my throat. "What you talking about, Marvella?" I shouted.

"Auntie died and was buried about three weeks ago," she said.

# The Politician

As Manny walked through the village, he saw the pages of exercise books pasted on walls and fences.

"Vote for Nathan," they said. "Nathan is for progress."

It was as if time had stood still and hope was truly eternal.

Standing alone in the gathering darkness, he heard the screeching of a loudspeaker like an intrusion in the silence of the night. He heard the first words that the teacher spoke, like a voice from his past. The words were the same and the voice was as hopeful as ever. In simple phrases, he lauded Nathan's intelligence and sincerity and the vast promise of his youth. Nathan was what the village needed; and he needed their support.

He heard Nathan begin in halting phrases. His voice quivered with earnestness as he accepted their trust and promised to give his life.

Manny did not have to listen to the words. In the far recesses of his mind, the words came out loud and clear. He remembered them too well. But he listened to the voice of sincerity as Nathan offered up his soul. At the end, when the village roared in acclamation, Manny stood quietly in the dark and wondered.

He had been a young man back then, idealistic and with high expectations; somewhat zealous for principle, but not assertively so. A clean-cut, pleasant boy, ardent and pure, he had no visions or ambitions beyond what he hoped to achieve to uplift the welfare of his village. He was a teacher, and he taught them,

ALICK LAZARE, a member of the former Dawbiney Literary Club, the Nature Island Literary Festival, and the Waitukubuli Writers Group, has self-published *Carib and Other Stories, Nature Island Verses, Pharcel: Runaway Slave,* and *Kalinago Blood.* He also contributed to Macmillan's anthology *Under the Perfume Tree,* and Commonwealth Education Trust's *A River of Stories.*

young and old, not only because that was his job, but more because he cared about them.

They admired his learning, and he, in turn, respected their down-to-earth wisdom. Together they had used their talents to build their small community into a pleasant, orderly place. Such was their respect and admiration of him that when the Party asked for a nomination to contest the general elections, they fought vigorously to make him their candidate.

The villagers were tired of the half illiterates that had represented them in the past. They were weary of men whose greatest talent was counting the under-the-table money that flowed into their pockets. Those men could barely read the ponderous speeches that public officials prepared for them to recite on occasions like the Independence Day Celebrations when they came to celebrate with their constituency. Although they had once been part of the village community, they could no longer understand the aspirations of those who had entrusted them with their welfare.

And so, the community had come to him. The priest and the teacher sat with him and spoke of his civic responsibility. They promised him their full support. In the end, he was persuaded to accept nomination as a candidate for the next parliamentary elections. The prospect had seemed daunting to him; but the priest and the teacher had carried him along the path that they had already cleared.

For many weeks, he trudged along the narrow village roads and spoke calmly to the smiling villagers. He entered their tiny wooden huts and smoking outdoor kitchens and listened to their hopeful voices. The priest and the teacher walked with him and gave support to his campaign. It was as if they had a personal stake in his success. Everywhere they went, the people listened and promised their vote.

Although his opponents came at night with bright floodlights and blaring speakers to harangue the people from the veranda of the largest rum shop, he remained calm. They shouted his name to the skies and spoke of his immaturity and inexperience, calling him the village idiot who had no knowledge of the world outside and no understanding of politics. But the villagers stayed in their homes and tried to sleep over the noise.

Manny's candidacy was officially set in motion six weeks before the date of the elections. The priest made an announcement at Sunday mass. From that time, the small community got busy with preparations. The teacher and the children wrote slogans on the pages of exercise books and posted them on the walls of their houses and on the doors of shops.

"Vote Manny. Vote for progress." They wrote the words in bright crayon colours, though many of them did not know exactly what progress meant. Everywhere he walked, the children smiled at him, and the grown-up people spoke with him respectfully as if he was already elected.

His opponents came with bright banners and promotional gifts which they spread all about the village. The people took them and applauded loudly; but they did not smile like they did for Manny.

Standing in the dark these many years later, Manny remembered it all. He remembered the night of the first elections when the results of the polls had been announced, the roar and the rising sound of triumph in the village. He could not believe that he had won, and won so convincingly. As in a dream, he had moved among his people, acknowledging their support. He had spoken simply and humbly to them and said that it was their victory, not his.

Afterwards, he sat with the people of the village and promised many things. He did not know then that it was in the nature of politics to promise. So he promised them his life.

"You have elected me," he told them. "I will always seek your counsel and your guidance. Always!"

They had believed him because they thought that he was an honest man and the people needed an honest representative.

In Parliament, he spoke with simple and quiet words as honest men do. He pleaded for improvements in his constituency and for the upliftment of the young people of his village. The Honourable Members applauded though they did not listen to what he had said.

Yet his village and his constituency remained untended. The roads were still unpaved and the water system inadequate. The children still had nothing to do after school. They remained idle in the fields around the village since there were no playgrounds for them. Still, the priest and the teacher stood by him and urged him to be patient and learn the art of politics. In time, he would learn how to make his voice heard, they said. He would learn how to make good things happen.

It was a veteran politician in the neighbouring constituency who finally showed him the ways of politics. He took Manny under his wings and introduced him to the ministers of government, to the leading bankers and merchants, to the manufacturers and the hoteliers, the operators and the racketeers. They all welcomed him as a young man with promise and commitment.

At first, the gifts came in the name of the village community and were specifically for playing fields and communal bath houses, for tidy village programmes and cultural events. The priest and the teacher were pleased with what he had done and did not ask how he was able to accomplish so much.

Manny's fame grew as money flowed to and from his pockets. The people came to him as if he was the fount of charity. He had never known that there was so much sickness and death and misfortune in his village. His scepticism grew; but still he gave. Yet the more he gave, the more that was demanded from him.

The priest and the teacher watched and wondered. They began to recognise the old ways of politics; but they remained silent.

One Friday afternoon, a brightly painted truck came into the village with speakers as tall as trees, electronic equipment, and miles of electrical wires which were installed in a disused banana shed. That same night, the booming sound of bouyon music roused the village to wakefulness. They all came and loitered and danced and drank the opening night's free alcohol. On Saturday night, carloads of visitors came, and the smell of weed and stale beer rose to the sainted ceiling of the church next door.

The teacher came and protested.

"Did Manny send you?" he asked.

"What Manny?' the bandleader replied.

"Our Manny," the teacher insisted.

"Oh, him! He in town with the big boys," he snorted, turning away.

On Sunday morning, the priest preached a sermon on the wages of sin and he made many allusions to Sodom and Gomorrah. The teacher told the story of the Pied Piper of Hamlin and cautioned his classes about the seductiveness of city life and the dangers of wayward living. But if they listened, they did not understand, especially as their parents said that the coming of the disco was a sign of progress. This they accepted because Manny was for progress.

Wherever Manny went, he was always attended by those who came to solicit help—advice, charity, jobs, security or patronage. In each village within his constituency, he was much sought after. He became their idol and was welcome in every home. Some of those who came were devious and intent on mischief, but he was not to know until later when truth did not matter anymore. Children still wrote in their exercise books: "Manny is for progress." Young ladies vied for his attention, some because he could open doors for them, others because they found him so personable. When he announced that he was to be married to the daughter of a shopkeeper, an assistant teacher from a neighbouring village, a decent girl whom everyone respected, the priest and the teacher were pleased. Still they thought that he should have been married in the village church instead of the Cathedral in the city with the pomp and the extravagance that his outside friends supported.

At first, his wife accompanied him to his many meetings and official functions. At home she sat with him in the evenings when the priest and the teacher came to visit. She would look at him with glowing admiration as he listened with patience and sought to explain to them what he had learnt about the ways of politics. That was before his new city friends intervened, surrounded him, and took him away. After that, he was never at home in the evenings anymore.

When elections rolled around again, Manny's new friends brought gaudy posters which they pasted on the church and school walls and on the walls of the disco and rum shops. They brought wide banners that they hung across the broken village roads and narrow grass-clogged paths. Loudspeakers sang his praises, and lively bouyon music played late into the night.

After that, his name was not mentioned at Sunday mass; and the children saved the pages of their exercise books for something else. The priest and the teacher stood aside and watched with heavy hearts as his army of supporters roamed the villages and spoke crudely of divisive politics.

His new friends convinced him that to cement the support of the men and women of his constituency he must befriend them and spread the benefits of patronage. And so, he slept many nights in strange beds and sat idly with men in village taverns. His licentiousness became legendary and his popularity spread from village to village.

They raised him on high when Manny's victory was declared. The government made him a minister. They said he deserved it because he had learnt the ways of politics.

He sat in his ministerial office the first day uncertain what to do. They brought him files and papers which he flipped through languidly. The paperwork grew into a huge pile that almost blocked his view of the world outside. The secretaries and other officials nodded and smiled. He thought he heard them snickering behind the walls of his office, but he was so lost in the welter of memos and minutes that arrived with questions for which he had no answers that he paid them little attention. He walked on deep carpet and sat on cushioned leather, and, for a while, felt uncomfortable with the strangeness of it all.

Those were the early days when he was learning the art of prevarication. In time, he learned to sift through the garbage dumped on him and to identify what was politically important. In the beginning, he listened to his advisors and dutifully read the pages of analysis and advice sent to him. Then he learned to give directions and hardly read the memos and minutes that sought to guide him. There was no questioning his importance. Manny's word became law, his whims became policy. He was praised because he was a man who got things done.

Manny's supporters waited in long queues at his office door. There were so many of them he couldn't be sure that he knew them all. Some he suspected had voted for the opposition, but he could not be certain. They came to him for land, for homes, for education, for family support and for hand-outs. He found many ways to accommodate their demands. He appointed them to statutory boards and public corporations. He brought them in as advisors because he thought he knew and trusted them. They were good because they were not bureaucrats who burdened him with too many papers, too much advice, or too many regulations. Together, they got things done, one way or another.

Investors, too, came in droves and sat patiently in his lounge waiting for him to admit them to his august presence. They came with fantastic proposals for profitable investments and promises of wealth for every citizen. In return, he was asked to give his endorsement in terms so convoluted that he was never sure what he was binding himself to. He received many gifts. Sometimes the gifts came even before he was asked to do anything.

It never occurred to Manny that there were many investors but no investments. As long as the gifts kept coming, he assumed that everything was moving in the right direction.

This was a very different world from his village. Here in the ministry, Manny was his own authority. His was to give and to take, so he took so that he could give. He thought he made his supporters dependent on him. But he did not yet understand the extent to which he was enslaving himself to them. Gently, but inexorably, they lured him onto the path of compromise. They pretended to love him even as they destroyed him.

The priest and the teacher faded into obscurity.

When the scandal eventually broke, he declared himself innocent. He said he was not aware of the hundred licensed but non-existent corporations or of the vast sums raised to finance them. Nor could he say what happened to the investors that vanished with so many millions of dollars. He never mentioned that he had ceased to read the memos and the minutes from his bureaucrats that cautioned restraint in his dealings with unsolicited and dubious enterprises.

He stood alone as the storm raged and engulfed him. His advisors had ceased to be, and the statutory boards and the corporations had fallen into disarray. The investors and their gifts were scattered with the winds. The queues at his office door dwindled and soon disappeared.

"I am an honest man!" he proclaimed.

Manny had said it so often that he came to believe it himself. Once, long ago, he knew himself to be honest, and most people had believed that he was; but that had been before.

"What I say is true!" he insisted.

He said it as if it was a decree announced from his high office, an indisputable statement of his will. That was how it was with him nowadays, so full of perverse delusions, so befuddled by the stubborn denial of reality. Nobody believed him anymore. Not like they did at the beginning.

When Manny returned to the village, the roads were still broken, the houses unlit and sanitary conditions primitive, it was as if time had stood still. The priest and the teacher still watched, but had given up hope.

He stood on the balcony of his village home and listened as the evening deepened and the fireflies, the crickets and the frogs awoke to their world of darkness. His wife had left the house a moment ago, so the lamps had not been lit as the night crept in.

She had left in silence, without saying where she was going. But he knew that she had gone to the village meeting and that she was too embarrassed to tell him that the villagers were supporting Nathan.

His mind went back to when it had started. He remembered the days of his youth when everything had been so simple and clean, when it had been clear in his mind what was good and what was immoral. The difference had been so obvious that it had not been difficult to choose. Back then, he was not aware of the thin line that separated good from immorality in the world of politics.

Manny could not pinpoint exactly when he had begun to drift away from his principles, or when his village world had quietly receded. The priest and the teacher had become distant, obscure, and redundant—irrelevant to his new political reality. Now he understood how much he had changed and how the people's adulation had transformed him. Twice they had chosen him to be their leader, and he assumed that they depended on him for their lives. But somewhere in the convoluted twists and turns of political manoeuvring, they had usurped his power of leadership. Now it was they who led. And they had led him astray.

As he listened to Nathan's voice rising to the skies, his earnest promises and self-assurance, Manny was filled with trepidation. He wondered how long it would be before they destroyed in Nathan that which they claimed to admire.

# The Double Blessing At Christmas

"Morning, Mrs. Osmonde. Walk carefully now. Those puddles on the road cover holes as deep as a coal pit."

"Thank you, Jacob. The village council is really lucky to have you as one of its workers."

"Say a prayer for me when you get there," the man responded, as he continued clearing the drain.

Isabella Osmonde promised to pray for him and set out on her twenty-minute walk to the church. It was the twenty-second of December, and that time of year and day made walking enjoyable, except when the rain decided to shower the land, as had happened the previous night. This was the seventh day of the Christmas novena. So far, Isabella had attended all the services and she wanted to complete the novena, so she heeded Jacob's warning as she walked. The previous week, a lady had broken her leg when she accidentally stepped in a puddle which hid the pothole beneath. She prayed fervently as she walked, asking for blessings on her son, her only child, and for her own forgiveness. If she deserved to be punished, she had already paid the price.

It had been a long and rough journey, but she had moved on. She was at a point now where she could accept reality and be at peace with herself.

She exchanged greetings with acquaintances after the service, and armed with an umbrella, left the church for the walk home. She took pleasure in the signs of Christmas preparations all around. The primary school was already closed, so some children were gathered under a tree, shelling pigeon peas for their parents. The occasional squeals she

DOROTHY LEEVY attended Convent High School and was the 1960 island scholar. She pursued studies at the University of Toronto, majoring in English literature. On her return home, she taught English and French. She was appointed the first lay principal of the Convent High School in 1983, and retired in 2004. She has published three collections of short stories.

heard from them indicated they found worms in the shells. Others were peeling sorrel. She had taken part in all those activities as a child, had joined in the exaggerated squeals when she saw a worm wriggling its way out of a pigeon pea or the shell. She noticed a table under a tree on an empty lot and knew that the meat from the animals killed would be sold there. Sounds of Christmas carols were heard from houses, most of which were already decorated with wreaths, garlands and other festive items. There were Christmas trees on some porches.

Isabella was grateful that she could enjoy and feel part of the Christmas spirit, and she returned the waves and smiles of the children.

Once she arrived home, however, a feeling of sadness overwhelmed her, and she had to sit while she fought it off. What was it the counsellor in the hospital had told her? "Each year, Mrs. Osmonde, as December twenty-third approaches, you may experience the pain, but you must not let it overpower you. You must forgive yourself."

Prior to receiving counselling, she had let the pain and self-torture take over. She had entered a period of steady decline, not eating, not sleeping, not caring, until her mind and body collapsed, resulting in hospitalisation. She was better now, a stronger person. Three years had elapsed since then.

She entered her son's room. It was almost eight years since Bruce had left, or rather, eight years since she had screamed and shouted at him to get out of her house and her life because she thought she was raising a man, and he obviously was not one. The room was as he had left it. His pictures of Juice Wrld, Kodak Black, and Tupac, though faded, were still on the wall. To Isabella, it was a sanctuary, but it was also a confessional area.

She sat on Bruce's bed and the memories came flooding back. Her husband's abandonment when her son was twelve was the first major disruption in what had seemed their normal lives. Timothy had given no indication that he was unhappy, that he was "different." Though he had moved with his partner to another village, rumours spread quickly on a small island. She had tried her best to ignore the shame and embarrassment, perhaps focused too much on her son, kept reminding him he was the man of the house, her protector. Did Bruce already exhibit certain signs which she had missed?

The counsellor assigned to her at the hospital had told her, "Any parent who goes searching the room of an eighteen-year-old must be prepared for anything found." She had been far from prepared that morning eight years ago when she entered her son's room while he was at a football game. She had gone to see if he had borrowed a pair of scissors which she kept in her room, but curiosity got the better of her and she decided to search through his dresser drawers. The sheet of paper with the typed words, found in the top drawer of his dressing table under some T-shirts was obviously part of a letter, but the rest of the letter was missing. She had taken up the sheet, and had read and reread, with anger mounting. He had come upon her while she was holding the paper. It was as though her anger at his father even, after all the years, and the shock she felt came to boiling point in her head and exploded.

"Isn't it enough that your father left us and went to live with someone young enough to be his son? So, you are like your father? You are no son of mine. Get out! Leave!" she had shouted.

Isabella still recalled seeing a few passersby lingering near the house, no doubt after hearing the shouting. She had gone to her room and closed the door. When she awoke the following morning, Bruce was not there. Anger and disappointment had kept her from calling him, though she had heard that he had moved in with a relative of his father, and then, a few months later, left the island. She assumed that his father's relatives in the United States had arranged for him to start college there.

She was fifty-two at the time, and she worked at the treasury in the second town. It was a half-hour drive to work from her home, the house she had inherited from her parents. She had moved there with Bruce after her husband left her. Shortly after she moved, Timothy had sold the house where they lived while they were married. It had been left to him by his parents, but he apparently did not wish to live in the area where he had grown up and was well known.

Though eight long years had passed, she remembered clearly the day after the incident. She could not get out of bed and had kept replaying the scene with Bruce. She had taken a few days off. She was aware of the looks of sympathy from her co-workers when she returned to work. In her unhappiness, she resented those looks, and as she had confessed to the counsellor at the hospital, she concluded that they thought her a worthless wife, whose husband had to find comfort in a same sex union, and whose son would probably do the same. The counsellor had tried to help her, and after hearing her account of the incident, had even instilled some doubt in her mind when he asked, "Are you sure the feelings expressed on the paper were those of your son?"

"I read the words," Isabella had replied. "Bruce wrote that he could no longer live a lie. It was there on paper. He wrote of the daily conflict which would kill him if he did not accept who and what he was. I was mother and father to Bruce after his father left us. He was aware of how I juggled work hours to attend PTA meetings, to be at home with him. Imagine how it hurt to read that he had to escape to liberate himself. I feel I have failed as a mother."

During her stay at the hospital, she had sessions every other day with the counsellor. When she continued blaming herself, he had asked her the following, "Do you think there is any mother who prays to God for her son to be gay? Suppose a mother discovers her son IS gay, is he less her son? Should her love suddenly be erased because he feels he cannot live a lie, cannot live with the conflict of pretending to be who he is not? Do you love your son, Mrs. Osmonde?"

For the first few years following Bruce's departure, she had been in a daze. The villagers who had known her deceased parents and who had known her as a child looked at her with pity. The children considered her as "the crazy lady." She overheard one child refer to her as such, as she passed near-by. She had been oblivious of the life around her then, left the gifts of food from the villagers on the porch, to be eaten by stray animals and rodents. She missed work frequently, and when she showed up, appeared to work mechanically. All that was before her stay at the hospital. It was Jacob who had noticed her on her porch where she had collapsed.

That was three years ago. Though the pain could never go away completely, Isabella considered herself a different person when discharged from the hospital from the one who had been admitted. She could accept the greetings and even gifts of the villagers. She considered herself healed, but "being healed does not mean the erasing of memories," the counsellor told her.

Isabella had taken his advice, and once she forced herself to take interest in the life around her, discovered it was easier to get through each day. She now took part in the celebrations and other events of the village. She had taken early retirement from work, though she was occasionally given work on contract. This kept her in touch with her colleagues whom she sometimes visited at the treasury or at their homes, as a few who had worked with her were still employed.

Yes, she had come a long way, and so her desire to complete the novena was not only to pray for her son, but also to thank God for her healing.

After coming from the church, after she had succeeded in calming her raging thoughts, she attacked her son's room with a fervour and vigour almost fanatical in its intensity. The following day, the twenty-third of December, would be another "anniversary," the eighth, to be exact, eight years during which she had not spoken to, or heard from him. She did not even know what he was doing, neither did she know his address. She was consoled by the fact that if he had been in any serious situations, if he were ill, Timothy himself or one of his relatives would have informed her.

She hardly slept that night. Sometimes, she wondered if she had imagined the hurt, along with a look of perplexity in her son's eyes, as she shouted recriminations and accusations at him.

After the novena service and mass the following day, Isabella drove to the capital, as she had done the past three years, to buy some gifts and some groceries and also to immerse herself in activities which would help her to "forget." She had overheard Jacob telling another worker that his pruning shears were not working properly, and she bought him some new ones. He was a very efficient worker, respectful, and generous with his time. She felt sad when she overheard some of the young men from the village referring to him as "Miss Jacob." She took it as a measure of how far she had come, because she could feel the injustice in the disrespect shown to Jacob by others.

As she walked through the stores, she tried her best to retain the peace she had felt at mass, and when she thought of her son, she prayed for his happiness and safety, wherever he happened to be. A cousin in Roseau named Lilian, who had returned to the island recently, had asked her to join her for lunch at one of the restaurants.

Both women drew admiring glances from patrons as they made their way to a table. They were about the same height, and though well into middle age, had succeeded in keeping that "middle-age spread" off their bodies.

As they relaxed and enjoyed their broth of smoked pork, yam and cabbage, they spoke of their respective deceased parents and other relatives they had in common, but tactfully avoided any reference to Bruce. Lilian and Isabella had attended the same primary school, were friends as well as first cousins. They saw each other more frequently now than when Lilian used to occasionally come from overseas to visit her parents in Dominica.

"You look so good, Bella," Lilian told her, calling her by the pet name her parents and other relatives used to address her. "Mamma wrote to me that it was as though you got a new lease on life after you left the hospital. I can tell you now how worried she was about you, how sad she felt that her own illness prevented her from being more of a help to you."

"Aunt Emma has remained my favourite relative," Isabelle responded. "Both your parents were sympathetic and generous to us. They always said I had provided the grandson for them to spoil."

There was a moment of strained silence after that indirect reference to Isabella's son.

Lilian broke it, saying, "I like the natural way you wear your hair. It enhances your beauty. But tell me, Bella, did you never think of remarrying after Timothy left you? You could have got an annulment, you know."

"Why go through the trouble of getting an annulment when I never had and still do not have any plans to remarry? Being a sole parent with a full-time job was sufficient responsibility, and I even failed in one of them," Bella replied.

"Come on, Bella, let's continue enjoying our meal and chat. I've heard nothing but praise on your behalf since I've been here, of the way you coped with work and as a parent, before you got ill."

"Before I lost it, you mean," Bella said. She felt good that she could treat the matter lightly and even laugh over it, and Lillian joined in the laughter.

Lilian accepted her invitation to visit her on Boxing Day and agreed to bring her daughter who would be visiting from England.

They left the restaurant and hugged as they reached the spot where Isabella had parked her vehicle.

She was happy. The outing and meeting with Lilian had done her good. She felt a measure of peace as she drove back to the village and arrived at her home. She opened the gate and saw the gift basket left by some villagers. She had accepted it gratefully every December twenty-third the past three years, a basket with fresh beef and pork, a yam, some sweet potatoes, pigeon peas, and sorrel. She felt a measure of shame when she thought of her selfishness before her "healing" when she had been so obsessed with her problems that she failed to accept the kindness of her neighbours, and left their baskets untouched in the yard.

With tears in her eyes, Isabella approached her house. As she stepped on the porch, she was aware of someone coming towards her. No, it could not be! She gasped, then screamed, and she opened her arms to embrace her son, Bruce. He, too, could not control his sobs. Then after a few seconds, she was aware of movement from the corner of the porch, and Bruce announced with pride in his voice, "Mom, it's time for you to meet my wife, Eloise, and your first grandchild, Beatrice Isabella Osmonde."

Isabella looked puzzled. "The letter you found in my drawer was from my father, not me," Bruce added quietly. "He and I never lost contact with each other. I just want you to know that I love you, Mom. I love you both."

# COVID-19 POEMS

# How Long Will This Last?

'Twas in the year twenty-nineteen
That deadly virus was first seen
No mercy it knew, no kindness was shown
Such evil in our world had never been known

All are affected from Prince to Commoner
The Preacher, the Doctor, the Political leader
Thousands of deaths are recorded each day
Despite plans to keep COVID-19 away

Kissing and hugging are now forbidden
Nose, eyes and mouth must now be hidden
Six feet apart, though lines are slow
Obey it not and under you go

A sore throat, a fever is how it attacks
Unfortunate souls, even those wearing masks,
Then a cough with no phlegm through the body
    will tear
Leaving victims weakened and gasping for air

Lungs turn to cement or feel like ice
Life to this predator becomes a game with dice
Ventilators, hazmat suits, N95 masks
Combat equipment every country grasps

O loving Creator how long will this last?
You are our refuge, our help, from ages past

DOROTHY LEEVY attended Convent High School and was the 1960 island scholar. She pursued studies at the University of Toronto, majoring in English literature. On her return home, she taught English and French. She was appointed the first lay principal of the Convent High School in 1983, and retired in 2004. She has published three collections of short stories.

# The Remains of Today

The best-laid plans will turn to dust
If tomorrow never comes.
Hopes and dreams will stall and rust
If the future is a ghost.

Experts tell us 'Stay at home,'
Some find it quite a curse.
But if a soul is home alone
That makes it even worse.

Fretful, lonely, desperate, hopeless:
These conditions need not be chronic.
Connected, active, open, selfless:
Shake well and drink the tonic.

But how to heal the whole wide world?
You ask the wizened sages.
Ah! Compassion, gratefulness, respect, and love,
Soothing balms throughout the ages.

And if tomorrow never comes?
Then we all must find a way
To gracefully, mindfully, humbly, cheerfully
Embrace the remains of today.

KRISTINE SIMELDA, co-founder of Waitukubuli Writers, has been a citizen of Dominica since 1995. Her short fiction has appeared in many regional and international journals, and her imprint, River Ridge Press Dominica, has self-published three adult novels and a novella for young adults. Her website is www.kristinesimelda.wordpress.com

# The Hearts of Men

The hearts of men are turning black
So day by day this world gets dark
As nation leaders Egos stack
The feeble masses slip through the crack
No one cares to think of peace
Or future costs to say the least
As western causes attack the east
They fuel the scourge which births the beast
The will of men are not the same
Death and destruction is now a game
With victory comes a string of Fame
So inhumane, it's just a shame
Global prices are soaring high
As food and fuel approach the sky
Weary parents all sit and cry
While children die in front their eye
Lands are burnt for oil and cash
Such precious trees reduced to ash
Oceans lined with tons of trash
Returned to shore by waves that crash
With weather patterns new and strange
And structures forced to rearrange
Seems man has forced his home to change
Like a dog that fleas have turned to mange
The hearts of men have lost their place
Now each hates the others face
Neighbors fight for land and space
Actions bound to end their race
Planet Earth is growing sick
From a cancer that is quite unique
Lest man should change his actions quick
His future here is clearly bleak

ERWIN MITCHEL is an unpublished poet and short story writer from the remote village of Dipax, Castle Bruce. A fire fighter by profession whose favourite way to unwind is to grab a paper and pen. Next to his fiancée and two beautiful children, his greatest goal is to publish his lyrical creations.

# World on Lockdown

Origin, Wuhan China
That COVID-19 thing
Forcing people to stay home
It was no time for bling

To try to stop the virus
Hubei province on lockdown
No more, wild animal shopping
Isolation all around

A Pandora's Box was open
This was indeed a threat
Little did the world know
It was about to sweat

Would you have imagined
San Francisco a ghost town?
No bars, no restos open
No night life to be found?

Then there's New York, the Big Apple
Many businesses in doubt
Leaving employees to grapple
Or to find a way out

The leadership of Governor Cuomo
Was indeed put to the test
Controlling this pandemic
Had him under duress

The situation became morbid
What a toll this virus took
Leaving New Yorkers grieving
With a grim outlook

President Trump upset with WHO
Threatened withdrawing funds
Citing incompetence and lack of vision
Of professionals on the ground

JERMAINIA COLAIRE-DIDIER lives in Dominica and has been a French lecturer for over 25 years. She holds a Masters' degree in Translation and Terminology and is passionate about the French language, as well as creative writing. Her dream is to publish her work in English and in French.

Who would have thought that Times Square
Would be a place of peace
No yellow, black and white taxi
No pedestrians on the street

And what about Champs Elysées
All cafes shut down
That famous busy avenue
With just joggers on the run

Trafalgar Square in London
Pigeons everywhere
No tourists to feed them
No taking selfies there

Las Ramblas in Barcelona
An avenue forlorn
No sight of human statues
No flowers, vendors gone

Let's talk about Italy
Gondolas all on strike
The canals clear as crystal
Playful dolphins in the night

In Rio de Janeiro
Copacabana beach lies still
No kaleidoscope of colour
No curvy tanned bodies, no thrill

The virus COVID-19
Set the whole world in a spin
With no vaccine to stop it
Blossomed into a whirlwind

The Caribbean was not spared
The virus brought its' dread
From Antigua to Trinidad
A few people laid dead

Thank God for Dominica
So far we're coping well
Let's hope this will continue
A success story to tell

Amazing how this virus
Travelling all around
Has mankind in a frenzy
And our planet on LOCKDOWN.

# Ode to Mother Earth

You needed this rest more than we did.
We have been destroying you and all you love
For as long as we can remember.

We have invented and reinvented,
Until we could invent no more.
We have polluted you over and over again.

Pumping waste into you
Until we could pump no more.
Now it's time for a purge.

Oh how things have changed.
The tables have turned.
It was time to turn a new page.

We have built walls so high
And skyscrapers so sublime
But they can't keep us from this demon.

We have the fastest jets
And the longest trains
Yet we can't run from this microbe.

We have had the loudest parties
And the fanciest of fashion
But still they're no match for this pathogen.

We were always on the go but
The only way we can win this war
Is to stay home and isolate.

Now you can breathe freely
Now your lakes, rivers and beaches are clear
And I can see the stars at night.

The only crime is if we come out of this
And not realise we had been the criminals all along
Killing the one thing meant to give us life.

ANELLA D. SHILLINGFORD is a member of Waitukubli Writers and an emerging writer. She is the author of *Bonfire*, a book of poems available on Amazon. She has a monthly blog, where she shares personal experiences with a unique spin. Anella is also a secondary school teacher in Portsmouth.

# Palm Sunday Lockdown

Palm fronds wave in the wind
A reminder of this Holy Day
In the Christian calendar
Held in high regard on the Nature Island.

No dressing up for service though
Instead, chicken dinners scent the breeze
As families carry on as best they can
Under extraordinary circumstances.

Children shout with glee
From secluded spaces
While a church service blares
From the porch next-door
Spreading hope and humility
To ears in close proximity.

Flycatchers flit to and fro
Beneath brilliant blue skies
And bold flowers
Display courageous attitudes,
Despite the drought.

Regardless of confined quarters
And no chance to openly celebrate
It's still a day to give thanks and praise
As Dominicans collectively strive
To keep the faith.

GWENITH WHITFORD is a freelance writer, editor, blogger and poet who currently resides in Canada. She became inspired to write poetry during the two decades that she lived full-time on Dominica. Her adopted country continues to be a winter escape, and she looks forward to further literary inspiration every visit.

# While Waiting

People darting to and fro
Seems like the whole world has somewhere to go!

At Number 1 we took the subway train
Bearing down upon each other—
From far and wide we came.
Crowds thronged Broadway streets,
Museums and Central Park—
As far as the eye could see
Bright lights lit the dark.
Brooklyn Bridge over-run by photographers
With cameras held high.
Tourists, civilians, merrymakers—
Onward and around in ignorant bliss
Not aware that in Asia something's amiss.

At Number 2 the first cases came ashore—
With a few planes full of travellers
Then more and more.
Bringing in people from every walk of life
To mingle among the masses—
A businessman, doctor, nurse, a housewife.
They came with a symptom like flue,
Fever and aches-
A corona virus—dangerous and new.
The uncertain fate of mankind began
When with a domino effect—
COVID-19 unleashed with a sinister plan.

At Number 3, the scientists already knew
That a race for a vaccine
Was too much to chew.
"A World Pandemic," observed WHO.
They declared the world unfit
To face this dangerous foe.
And so here I am behind closed doors—

ANDREA ANTHONY DIB's love for writing started in primary school, having read nearly every book in the library. She has used her lyrics to participate in DOMFESTA (Dominica Festival of Arts) (1 of 10 finalists) and Dominica Calypso Competition, organised drama and dance concerts, and is a member of her church's Music Ministry.

'Self-quarantine and social distancing'—
Terms most never heard before.
Lying low in my 'new norm'
I shift, re-adjust and wait
For the end of COVID-19 and a brand new morn.

# De Life Changer

Who would have thought
That today you could a walk into a bank
Wearing dark shades, hand gloves and a mask?
Never could such a ting happen in times past!
Is not a hold up for you carry no gun
But if you start to cough every man jack, teller and all
  would run.
Yes me bredder, COVID is de life changer.

Who would have imagined riding on a bus from de
  countryside
And the driver gone town and he passengers pan de
  roadside
Cause he can only carry one in a row, so no more
  squeeze.
This ting so bad that I hear in Jamaica a man get beat
  on a bus because him sneeze,
And then they throw him off as a unwelcomed stranger
Because of COVID-19 de compelling life changer.

Who would have thought
We would have to stand six feet apart anywhere and
  everywhere?
And if by mistake you forget your social distance
And happen to touch somebody for instance
Out come the hand sanitiser, is like you have a cancer.
Is not dey fault, is de result of COVID de life changer.

Who would have ever thought that tings would be so
  strange
Lock down everywhere, State of Emergency, curfew for
  months.
With school, college, church, supermarket, restaurant,
  hotel, pharmacy all fully or partially closed
And almost everybody confined and compelled to doing
  tings on line.

JULES PASCAL has won numerous awards for both English and Creole poetry. He is a former primary school teacher, a retired youth development worker, and an accredited Minister of the Gospel. In 1988, he co-authored a book of poems, *Pawol Kweyol,* and published *The Ravages of a Monster Storm on a Tropical Island* in 2019.

Shop on line, school online, pray online, market online,
some even try party online.

As for shopping dem prefer payment by card cause dey
fraid to take any virus infected cash

But is de COVID dat change we life and make it so
harsh.

An who would have thought that the Creator would
allow such a ting to take place

Super powers who always showed their might, now
COVID have them in fright and flight.

All dem senseless wars now come to halt, faced with one
common enemy

Now all dem soldiers employ in funeral homes, as hearse
drivers to carry and bury the dead.

All them developed countries who throw out de Creator
and scorn His face

Now falling pan dem knees, with hands in de air and
asking for His grace.

It had to take COVID to show de real life changer.

None would have thought that one virus could have
blast the whole world so strong

That man can't find answers, so everyone is asking Papa
God for how long?

Long enough to effect so much change,

Change in economy, change in philosophy, change in
policy, change in theology.

Change in our methodology, change in every country.

Everything and everyone will change

De COVID itself and its effect must change,

But not The Creator who made change

**For He is de only real life changer**